BIRD AREN'T REAL

D.T. ROBBINS

A MAUDLIN HOUSE BOOK

MAUDLIN HOUSE

maudlinhouse.net
twitter.com/maudlinhouse

Birds Aren't Real
Copyright © 2023 by D.T. Robbins
ISBN 978-1-7370222-6-8

For Kam

Acknowledgments

I'd like to first thank my wife, Alyssa, for…literally everything. I love you. Thank you to Drew Hawkins, Kyle Seibel, Lauren Theresa, Mallory Smart, Bulent Mourad, Greg Chandler, Tex Gresham, Kurt Kroeber, Kris Hall, and Aaron Burch. Thank you to the editors of the journals and magazines in which many of these stories originally appeared.

Table of Contents

Icebreakers

The little cubes where their faces go are black and reads their names the first few minutes of the virtual team meeting. Everyone waits to see who'll reveal how much fatter they've gotten since the last virtual team meeting. One little cube forgets to mute itself. A magnificent fart rips its way through laptop speakers from east coast to west coast, in three different time zones. Nice. No one says anything. No one ever says anything. The asshole whose asshole chose violence is left in ignorance of his newfound legacy. Thanks, Paul.

A flicker of light opens up one of the little cubes. Margaret and her flat face and purple hair sits in front of her beachy Hawaiian background. She holds a coffee mug that reads: Grrl Boss. Other faces break out of the other little cubes. The guy with the tank top fixes his hair. The girl with the pixelated face shoos her cat off her desk. Everyone else just tries not to be noticed. Tries to make it through the next hour and a half. The next work week. The next lifetime of monotony and swift disappointment.

"Happy Monday," Margaret says.

Half-smiles and thumbs-ups.

"How was everyone's weekend?"

More thumbs up. More half-ass smiles.

"Well, I hope you all had a wonderful holiday break. Welcome back! I don't know about you guys, but..." and on and on and blah blah what the fuck ever, am I right?

Margaret decides the best way to start the meeting that no one wants to be at is do an icebreaker no one wants to participate in: two truths and a lie. By the end, no one knows if so and so is lying about going to jail or if they changed their mind at the last minute and said that was actually a lie, two people are definitely fucking even though they live nowhere near each other, but you can totally tell, and Dan has hemorrhoids.

"That was fun," Margaret lies.

Thumbs up.

Margaret asks each person, starting with Dan, to go through what's on their task list for the week and give an update on anything else that might be pending or past due. One by one they take their turns. Do an evaluation of user analytics. Data privacy updates. Send out invites for staff recognition luncheon. Prepare the budget for the upcoming fiscal year. Email this person. Email that person. Revise whatever. Inventory that. Jesus Christ!

Margaret turns her turd-brown eyes on Cleo. "Alright, Cleo. What d'ya got?"

Cleo stares back at their collective unenthusiastic gaze. She coughs a little cough. A cute little cough. Aw. It's sweet. Like a kid's cough. She coughs again. A little more bass on that one. Once more with feeling. She hacks and hacks, never blinking. Her lungs deflate, collapse a little with each hack until she starts to cackle. Her eyes stretch and expand into two hollow abysses. From each socket reaches a skeletal hand, melting flesh going drip drip drip off the bones. Her tongue falls out of her mouth and a little man with an orange jumpsuit and a chainsaw slide down onto her desk. The laughter shoots like arrows through the speakers. Everyone covers their ears, starts crying tears of blood and oil. Smoke rises from behind Cleo. Slowly. Like a lion or cheetah or some other big fucking cat stalking its prey. The smoke wraps its gray arms around Cleo. A hug and a squeeze.

The other faces in the other cubes watch in horror. They watch each other watching in horror. They watch themselves watching in horror. They watch as the smoke spreads from one cube to the other. The little man in the orange jumpsuit with the chainsaw pops up and slits every throat in every cube. Margaret's head comes clean off, rolls onto the keyboard. One bloodshot eyeball staring into the camera on her screen. Looking good, Margaret.

Cleo's cackle breaks the sound barrier. Her skin boils and bubbles and goes drip drip drip. Flames go whoosh all around her until the whole cube is like the video of that fireplace burning at Christmas time. Happy holidays! Paul's asshole is ripped from his body. One head explodes, leaving goo all over the camera. Another head. Then two more. The little man with the chainsaw carves up bone and flesh. In unison, the cubes sink below the earth as hell reaches up to grab them and eat their souls and…

Did anyone remember to record this meeting?

Following Signs

I mean, I've always been a believer in signs. Why wouldn't I? I think the key is to just stay open-minded and follow them once they show up. You never know where they'll take you. Sky's the limit or something, you know?

So, I'm riding the train on my way to work when a bright beam with my name written on it shoots through the car and circles back, hanging a few feet in front of me. Well, obviously, I call my boss and say sorry something came up, I'm not able to make it in today, thanks for understanding. It's a few stops before the beam leads me off the train. We go above ground where a taco cart is giving out free churros. See? Score! But it gets better. It takes me through a park where this hipster guy is busking. He's really good, too. He asks if anyone has any requests. I shout out Mr. Jones by Counting Crows and, what do you know, he asks me to sing it with him. Needless to say, I sing the shit out of that song and we pull a pretty good haul. End up with thirty-two bucks each just from that song.

I'm thrown for a loop when the beam takes me to my office. I think maybe it's just messing with me but sure enough we head inside to my cubicle. I turn on my computer and do a solid two hours of work and another solid two hours of watching old WWF videos on YouTube. When my boss walks by around noon and sees I'm back, he commends me for my work ethic and my willingness to push through difficult circumstances in order to get the job done. He tells me he'll be keeping me in mind the next time someone is up for a big promotion.

After work, I follow the beam to a bar down the street. Some of my other coworkers are already there ordering Guinness.

"Who told you we were coming," the IT guy asks.

"Oh, no one, really. I just had a hunch this was a good spot to be," I say.

"Well, that's a little weird," the receptionist says, looking at the IT guy with a side-eye.

I apologize for intruding and follow the beam to an empty booth at the other side of the room. The beam tells me to try the French dip and I do and it's good. I watch as a few more coworkers pile in at the bar, laughing and drinking and flirting with each other. The receptionist keeps looking over at me. I look at the beam but the beam isn't moving so neither am I. I'm faithful to my beam. I order a few whiskey and ginger ales and listen to whatever punk band is playing on the jukebox.

Her glances turn into staring. Before long she's over at my table, asking me how long I've been with the company and other work-related shit like is my degree in editing and do I plan on staying or changing careers in the next few years. I don't know the answer.

"You never come out with us. Why'd you come today," she asks.

"Do you believe in signs?"

"One time my sister heard Bruno Mars singing from her toaster," she says.

"Really?"

"Yeah. So, we went to one of his concerts the next month. He pulled her up on stage. Now she does real estate and she's super rich. Does that count?"

"I think so."

"Do you have a crush on me?"

The beam starts moving toward the door. "I gotta go."

She asks if she can come with me.

"Yeah, but I don't really know where I'm going."

"That's ok."

I throw the money I'd made from busking on the table.

I'm having a hard time following the beam and she's having a hard time following me because we're both drunk and the beam is moving quickly. I trip over some raised cement on the sidewalk and fall flat on my face, cut my chin all up. She tells me we should slow down but the beam is still moving so I say no way, we've got to follow the signs. She laughs and thinks I'm joking but I'm dead serious. This is the best day of my whole life. We're holding hands and running across the street and dodging cars and passersby and laughing when they honk or tell us to watch where we're fucking going, assholes!

The beam takes us a few blocks or so to a Krav Maga dojo. It's packed with women in their mid-forties who look mean as hell. We sign up for a free trial and get our asses handed to us. I watch her get thrown across the room just as I'm blacking out from the chokehold I'm in. I think she might be the one. Neither of us sign up for any lessons when it's over but the ladies say we can have a couple free t-shirts since we were such good sports about our beatdowns.

It's dark now and the beam is the brightest it's been all day. My name floats across the sky like my very own honkytonk sign. We talk about growing up, the nineties, the strangest places we've had sex. For her, it was in the back of a UPS store. For me, a cave.

"Like, a cave-cave?"

"Yep. Like, Batman's cave."

"Were there any bats?"

"I don't think so, but I wasn't paying attention."

"That's disgusting," she says, laughing.

"I've seen worse."

"Uh huh. I've had a really great time with you today."

"Today's been the best. But I haven't been entirely honest with you," I say.

"Shit. You're a psycho killer, aren't you?" She puts up the sign of the cross with her index fingers.

"Maybe. But, you asked me earlier if I have a crush on you. I kinda do."

"I knew it," she says.

I lean down and kiss her long and hard. Her lips still taste like Guinness. I like it. She seems to like the kiss. That's good. I always worry I'm a shitty kisser. When it's over I tell her how I like her eyes and her nose because it's so small. We keep following the beam. She's definitely the one.

She squeezes my hand when she realizes the beam has brought us to a cemetery. I tell her don't worry, it'll be okay, let's go. The beam zig-zags through a bunch of plots and stops at one about fifty yards away. Her arms wrap tight around mine.

"Ugh. This is weird," she says.

"I guess."

At the point where the beam stopped, there's an empty grave. Dirt is piled up next to it. I feel her tense up. She's shivering, staring at the tombstone.

"That's my name," she says. "The dates are wrong, but that's my name."

"Oh, yeah. Weird."

Oi

I'm hungover again, puking in the grass when someone screams oh shit! I push through the crowd, see Oi lying face down on the quarter pipe. I kick him, tell him get up, quit fucking around.

The ambulance pronounce Oi dead. The cops tell everyone to go home. I show the cops my balls. They chase me, beat the shit out of me, say the only reason I'm not going to jail is because they don't want to clean up when I puke in their car. I smile all bloody. Haha.

In the bowl, I hear someone's trucks on the rails. Oi's ghost is skating. He looks up, flips me off, tells me come skate. He's all shiny and totally ripped.

I ask him how he got so jacked. He says he always wanted big muscles and that God was super chill and gave him some, no questions asked.

I ask, "What's heaven like?"

"I mean, it's pretty lit. You basically do whatever you want all day, party all night. I can fly now. Watch." Oi lifts off the ground, board and all, goes sailing through the sky, pops an ollie on some clouds. Rad. When you die, he says, even though it's only like a couple of seconds here on earth, everything in the afterlife is sped up by, like, a thousand or something, so he's grown up a lot, totally matured. I call bullshit. He takes out his wallet, unfolds his doctorate degree: PhD in Enochian Literature. He lists off all the celebrities he's met, tells me Kurt Cobain is a super nice dude but if you touch his guitars, he'll fuck you up because he's a kung fu master now and traded all his flannels and ripped jeans for a karate gi.

We skate all night and talk about chicks he's already banged or wants to bang in heaven and the ones he thinks I should and shouldn't bang here on earth.

I break down, start bawling my eyes out. "I miss you, dude. This place fucking sucks without you. I hate everyone. I don't wanna fuck any chicks. I'd rather skate and get drunk with you all day, every day, like today before you died. Remember?"

Oi puts his hand on my shoulder. Everything around us turns to liquid, melts to the floor, erases, until we're standing in a white room. Jason Molina from Songs: Ohia stands in the corner with his acoustic guitar, starts singing Just Be Simple. Oi doesn't say a word, just smiles, stares at me for the whole song. Tears keep running down my face. I love this song. On the wall, a movie plays: Oi's life, had he not died. It goes by fast and it's sad because he looks so happy.

There's a wife, a kid, some grandkids, a house, a job that he bitches about but is super proud of, a cancer scare, retirement, and it ends with him dying when he gets run over by a bus.

After the movie, I ask, "Where was I?"

"You were there," he says.

The world drips like paint down the white walls until we're back at the skatepark.

"I didn't see me."

"It wasn't your movie."

"Oh, yeah."

"You're gonna be fine, dude," he says. "Trust me."

I start crying again, put my head on his shoulder. I wait for him to punch me, tell me stop being a pussy. He doesn't. He lets me cry for a long time. Probably a couple decades worth according to his watch.

"I gotta go," he says.

"Ok. You suck," I tell him.

"I love you, dude. See ya later."

Electricity buzzes through the streetlamps. The sidewalk has its own gravity. I'm glued to the earth, waiting until I've done my time.

Watch

I find my watch in a ball pit at the McDonald's down the street after everyone disappears.

Oh, yeah. Everyone's gone. Ack! Boo! Hiss! Anyway, we go everywhere, do everything together. BFF4L. We talk about our favorite and least favorite cults, tell each other ghost stories, cry when Macaulay Culkin dies in My Girl. You get it. It's nice to have a friend. It's nice to have anyone, really.

Today, my watch tells me it's time to visit all of the graves.

"All of them?"

"All of them."

I throw some trinkets into my backpack to leave on the tombstones, then rollerblade across the bridge to the cemetery. One of the lampposts has fallen over since the last time we visited, cracked Ellen Shoemaker's tombstone in half. I ask my watch if that's a bad omen or something.

It says, "Ellen Shoemaker is dead. Can't get any worse."

I leave her an oven mitt anyway.

Toy trucks. Ballpoint pens. Picture frames. Blankets. Aspirin. Each grave gets something different. If I were dead, I might appreciate someone leaving a lasagna recipe for me, or a picture of Chris Farley. It'd be nice to be remembered.

We're almost out of trinkets when my watch stops me. "Wait," it says.

I wait. "What's wrong?"

"Underneath you. Put me down."

I put my watch on the ground, face-side up.

It tells me something is still alive under the dirt.

I use a spade nearby, start shoveling. The handle's rotted, breaks in half. About an hour later, I hit the casket. We open it, find a woman inside. She's alive, alright. Chest rising, falling. Eyes flitting back and forth behind their lids, deep in REM. I'm afraid to wake her.

"Hello," my watch says, volume ten.

She smiles and asks, "How long have I been out?"

I hand her the last trinket in my bag: measuring tape. My watch tells me to bring her home with us.

Back home, we're all three sitting at the kitchen table, eating buttered toast and drinking Rainier. "I'm Reggie," she says.

"Nice to meet you, Reggie," says my watch.

I try to say it's also nice for me to meet her but choke on some crust.

"Chew your food," my watch reminds me.

It's crowded at the table. Reggie chews her toast and slurps her beer loud. Chomp. Chomp. Chomp. Gulp. Gulp. Gulp. Like, we get it, you haven't eaten in a long time. Be cool, though.

My watch says it wants Reggie to wear it, you know, to make sure Reggie is okay. Check her blood pressure and cholesterol and brain waves. Turns out, she's perfectly fine. Congratulations, you're not actually dead!

"Can I have my watch back now?"

Reggie spends the night asking questions about the world, asking how long it's been this way, asking why we go to the graves, why the trinkets, what's this, where's that celebrity, blah blah blah yak yak yak barf. She asks if we've ever found anyone else in the cemetery who wasn't fully dead. I tell her no, she's the only one, go to sleep. She falls asleep smiling. I stay up all night tossing, turning, tossing, turning.

The next day it rains, hot and blue as usual. Reggie won't shut up about how she's never seen blue rain before. I tell her maybe next time she shouldn't get buried alive and maybe she won't miss the apocalypse and all the cool shit it offers. Then, I won't have to answer her lame questions over and over and over again. I guess that was the wrong thing to say or something because the next thing I know she's sobbing with a paper bag over her head. I say I'm sorry, offer to take her to a really cool place my watch and I found that we like to go to when it's raining outside. She says okay but she's keeping the bag over her head. I say whatever, let's just go.

"It used to be a factory where they made ice cream and cheese," my watch tells Reggie. We watch blue rain cascade down the hole in the roof, filling the swimming crater below. I run up to the third story, take off my clothes, tell Reggie to watch this. Kowabunga!

"Be careful," she yells.

I cannonball into the blue rain water and sink down, down, down. The water feels like a bath. My watch pulsates, pushing all the gunk out of its crevices. Here we are, me and my watch, wrapped in the blue abyss of elsewhere, a beautiful silence, an escape from above. Above, where it's truly empty. I stretch my arms, weightless, float to the top.

As soon as my head bobs above the water I hear Reggie's shrill scream. Her voice bounces around the steel walls. I panic, thinking she's hurt but nope, she's screaming at me and telling me never ever, ever do that again to her. Never scare her like that. Never do anything that selfish again. Never ever, never ever.

"Who will take care of me if you drown?" she asks between dry heaves.

"I wasn't gonna drown," I say. "I know what I'm doing, okay?"

"Asshole." She throws the paper bag in my face, storms off.

When we get back home, Reggie is sticking a fork in the electrical socket but the electrical socket doesn't work so she's stabbing and crying and nothing is happening. My watch starts playing a hypnotic, ambient soundscape noise, whales or thunderstorms in space or something like that. She stands up, wipes her eyes, starts swaying side to side. I wonder if maybe this is a side effect from being dead but not really being dead, just stuck in a coffin for too long. Loss of oxygen or whatever can really screw with your brain and I'm thinking that might be the case here. Reggie sashays over, grabs my hips. We're dancing to the sound of whales fucking somewhere beyond our galaxy and it's nice.

"Are you okay?" I ask.

"No one is okay. We're all beautiful deaths dying over and over in an infinity symbol at God's slaughterhouse. I just want to pull the lever for once is all."

I understand.

That night she sleeps in my bed. We have sex and it's all very robotic but she says it still feels good. When I come, she bites my shoulder, breaks skin. Blood drips down on my pillow.

She tells me she killed one of her brothers once and that I sort of remind her of him but I'm not as good looking.

"It was the 90s and everything was so colorful," she whispers in my ear. "You could walk into any coffee shop and order a cup of rainbow, no problem. I told all my friends that my favorite band was Failure, but it was really Sixpence None the Richer. She's All That is my favorite movie.

I tell her how sorry I was that everything was so different now, that maybe it'll end up being a fresh start for her like it kinda was for me. She smiles, turns over and goes to sleep. My watch plays "Kiss Me" and I fell asleep too.

The door is left open, the sound of the wind banging it over and over and over into the wall wakes me up. My sheets are soaked in sweat, my pillow dark red from all the blood. Reggie is gone. My watch is gone. The bread in the kitchen is gone. She left the toaster. I put on my rollerblades, head to the cemetery, find the hole I'd dug Reggie out of. Blue rain falls as I lay my head on the silk padding of the coffin and shut the lid. I close my eyes, wait to be found.

Merry Christmas From The Moon

They set the rotary telephone and the bucket of fried chicken on the table. She'll call tonight, they say. Why wouldn't she? Living on the moon shouldn't stop her from calling and telling her parents Merry Christmas and I love you. Mom is wearing that dress shaped like a Christmas tree, already halfway through a packet of Kleenex. Dad's drunk, his red and green tuxedo stinks of eggnog. Sure, she should call. Probably will. But what if she doesn't? She called last year, didn't she? Did she? Do you remember? No, do you? How does time pass on the moon?

Ring. Ring. Ring. A drunk cousin. "Merry Christmas, Raymond," Mom says, "tell Estelle we said hello."

Dad turns on the radio. All Mariah Carey wants for Christmas is you and all they want is their daughter and all anybody wants is someone they can't have. Dad makes himself a Christmas Cheer: Baileys and Bourbon and milk. Mom pours a glass of wine. They drink, fill up, drink.

"Wanna watch a movie?" Mom asks.

"Which one?" Dad asks.

"The one with all the people in the airport. It's got that guy from the kidnapping movies," Mom says.

"I don't wanna watch that one," Dad says, making his whatever-numbered Cheer.

"But we used to watch it all the time."

"Why?" Dad asks.

"Well, fuck you, then."

Neither of them got any presents for the other this year. Or last. Or the year before that. Or for the past fifteen years. But the tree is up in the living room and the lights are up outside the house and the radio is playing and Dad asks Mom to dance and they do. Mom starts crying. Dad asks what's wrong and Mom tells him how nothing's felt right since she left for the moon and Dad says, I know, I'm sorry. Mom asks if Dad thinks she'll call and Dad says he can only hope, but hope doesn't always amount to anything.

Ring. Ring. Ring. "Yes, Estelle, we already talked to Raymond. Yes, we know he's drunk. Goodnight. Merry Christmas to you, too."

It doesn't snow in Phoenix but the dust floating around their daughter's room gives Mom and Dad the feeling that they're walking through a winter wonderland. She hasn't been here in so long. She hasn't called in so long. Mom's packet of Kleenex is empty. Dad takes off his t-shirt, hands it to Mom. They make out on her bed, fall to the floor. Get busy.

Dad wipes the sweat off his forehead and chest and gut.

Mom watches, smiling. "We can't tell her we did this in her room," she says.

Dad laughs. "Why not? Serves her right, being gone for goddamn ever."

Mom laughs, then cries. "Why would you say that?"

There's grease all over the tablecloth. The bucket of chicken is gone. Dad is sprawled out on the couch watching the movie about kidnapping with the guy from that movie about the people in the airport.

Mom stands in front of the television. "Listen up, asshole!"

Dad turns the television up.

Mom sits in front of the screen, blocking his view.

They stare at each other as long as it takes for the good guy to beat the shit out of fifty bad guys and find the main bad guy that he still has to beat the shit out of.

Dad asks, "Why are you like this?"

"Because you let her go."

"It was her or you," Dad says.

The baddest bad guy gives his monologue on the TV. Mom asks, "What the hell is that even supposed to mean?"

"Neither of you could stand each other. It was time she got out on her own, did her own thing, grew up. And I missed my fucking wife. Now she's gone and you're meaner than ever. I lost. Big time. So, leave me alone while I watch the man on the TV blow shit up."

WHAM!'s Last Christmas is on the radio. Mom hums along, pulls out some cookies from the oven. They're expired, but she thinks they'll taste fine. She opens the window to let out the heat, listens to the breeze against the wind chimes out back. Or maybe it's Santa and his sleigh.

Dad lights a cigarette on the front porch, watches the stars and satellites sail across the sky. Or maybe they're reindeer.

Mom walks out with the plate of cookies, sits in the chair next to Dad. They eat, drink milk.

"I miss being Santa," Dad says.

"Me too."

Ring. Ring. Ring. Ring.

The moon pours out what little light it has left to give. Their eyes fixed, knowing it won't last forever.

Harry Pulls Up Weeds

Harry pulls up the weeds in his garden. The weeds keep suffocating the lavender flowers Harry has been trying to grow for the past few months. Harry pulls at the weeds with his good arm, the only one he has left, the one his ex-wife didn't take in the divorce settlement. His right arm.

The weeds pull back. Harry goes underground. Harry screams, scared shitless. AAAGHHGHHARERLKARGAA*@$%*!!!!

Bye, Harry!
Hi, Harry!

Welcome to your new home. It isn't much different from the world above except all the colors are inverted and capitalism is dead. Harry doesn't mind at all. Harry tried capitalism, tried opening a convenience store in his previous world. It left him bankrupt and bored and divorced. Ugh. Bummsville, right? Yeah, Bummsville. That's what he calls his old world. He doesn't have a name for the new world yet. It'll come in time, Harry thinks.

Harry finds an apartment cheap, much cheaper than he would have found back in Bummsville. Yay! This apartment has carpet that sways and tickles your toes. Spiders come at night and sing you to sleep if you want them to. The fridge is always stocked with Miller Lite and the bread never goes stale.

Harry finds a job as a taxidermist. They stuff everything here: wolves, cats, chickens, couches, pinecones, dead uncles, people in comas. Harry is good at stuffing things. It reminds him of how he dealt with his divorce back in Bummsville.

Harry's neighbors smoke crystal meth and yell at each other all day. Uh oh. Harry's neighbors put a roll of aluminum foil in their microwave, set the apartment complex on fire. Everyone runs out screaming and crying and dancing dances of mourning and sorrow. Harry straps his fridge to his back, barely makes it out alive. Worth it, he says. Free beer forever!

Harry has to move into a trailer park. None of these neighbors smoke crystal meth or scream at each other throughout the night. These neighbors are all part of a cult. They mostly keep to themselves, though they invite Harry to their weekly meetings. Harry says no thanks, he's not religious. Is this what all those coexist bumper stickers were talking about back in Bummsville?

A tornado hits the park. It's beautiful, made of glitter and laughter. Harry always wanted children. Harry cries as he watches all the trailers get destroyed. All except Harry's.

Everyone moves in with Harry. All 350 cult members. Harry doesn't mind so long as they stay the hell out of his beer and bread. No exceptions! Harry charges the cult ten pies a month to stay with him in his trailer. The cult calls him a slumlord, shits on his couch, moves out.

The cult secretary, Daphne, stays behind. Daphne bakes as many pies as Harry wants.

Harry and Daphne fall madly in love. Daphne proposes to Harry with a diamond arm to replace the arm his ex-wife in Bummsville took from him in their divorce settlement. Yes! Yes! A thousand times yes!

Daphne gets pregnant, gives birth to a fiddle leaf. The fiddle leaf rebuilds the trailer park, becomes mayor of the trailer park. Crime goes down. Yay!

Harry and Daphne move to New Orleans, live in the French Quarter, eat beignets all day everyday, hell fucking yes! Harry keeps taxiderming because he likes the quiet and now he has his diamond arm and can do the work doubletime. Harry becomes a world famous taxidermist, even gets his own television show. Congrats, Harry!

Daphne dies at the age of 256. Harry hasn't aged a day. At Daphne's funeral, Harry buries the diamond arm that she gave him when she proposed.

Harry retires, becomes a carpenter. He knows nothing about carpentry. Harry builds his first house with his one good arm, the only one he has left. His right arm. The house is beautiful, made of sunshine and oak.

A thousand years go by. Harry sleeps through most of them. The fiddle leaf becomes president. The USA burns to the ground, killing everyone and everything, including Harry. All Americans return as ghosts. The USA is the only 100% ghost-occupied country in the world. Harry travels cross-country to see if he can find Daphne's ghost. But she's gone. Gone forever. Farewell, again, my love. Kiss kiss.

Harry comes home from his road trip, goes out into the yard, sees weeds killing his lavender. Harry pulls up the weeds. The weeds pull back.

Bye, Harry!

Hi, Harry!

Welcome to the after-afterlife.

Harry transforms into a mountain. He's covered in lavender. The wind sounds like Daphne's voice. Harry watches the sun hang in suspended animation, almost and never setting for all eternity.

The Leg

If you cut my leg and peel away the muscle, there's a family living inside. Dad aims to be a voodoo priest. He spends most of his time exorcising the spirits that try to amalgamate with them from the other parts of my body, the meaner parts. The boy siphons rye from my veins, the girl uses them as swings — little cuties. Mom tells herself not to worry, that everything'll be a-okay.

At night, when they're asleep, I peel back my leg and have a cocktail or two with her. She asks if she can step out for a moment, just to stretch. I tell her no, stay inside where it's safe, where there's plenty to do. It's hell out here, I say. Remember when I found you? The world zigged across the galaxy when it should have zagged. Now we're all traveling down a black hole, transmogrifying into spaghetti noodles. At least you've still got your family, I say.

I wish I could switch with her but one of us has to be the leg.

Bones Gets Some Sleep

Bones got the name Bones because his mom always said that when Bones slept, he slept like a sack of old bones or something like that. But Bones is having a hard time sleeping these days. In fact, Bones can't sleep at all. Bones has insomnia. Yeah, insomnia. Poor Bones. What a drag, right? Night after night it's the same thing: Bones gets in bed, tells himself that tonight is the night he'll finally get a good night's rest but, lol, guess what? Nope. The ceiling swirls above, making sounds like a garbage disposal filled with ice. Coyotes yap and howl and kill his neighbors' pets outside. His sheets feel like fiberglass, itching and cutting and oh my god. He's tossing tossing tossing turning turning turning because, Jesus Christ, of fucking course he is.

Bones tries Melatonin, therapy, weed, CBD oil, muscle relaxers, acupuncture, meditation apps with those ambient soundscapes on his phone, you name it. He tries figuring out what was causing his insomnia. Was it seeing that dead body on the Gravitron when he was a kid? Was it his crippling fear of the state of Idaho? Was it the time he pissed his pants waiting in line at Best Buy? All horrific, but not the cause. He stops trying to figure it out and you should, too. It is what it is.

Then the spiders come, hundreds of them, tapping their legs on his window. It sounds like rain. They sing in a chorus of smoky voices, like Amy Winehouse or Chan Marshall or early Tom Waits. They sing the theme song from Twin Peaks, they sing "Frank Sinatra" by Cake (they get really into it during the *flies and spiders get along together* line). Before long, old Bones is out like a sack of old bones. He dreams of darkness, straight up blackness, nothingness. He wakes to find the spiders scattered when the sun comes up. Bones checks the clock on his microwave every hour on the hour to see if it's almost sundown. He spends the day cleaning his apartment, looking for the spiders, hoping to find them hiding in all the crevices and all the dark places. But they aren't there or anywhere he looks. So sad, super sucks. Night comes. Bones takes a shower, drinks a beer, cries, gets in bed, stares at the ceiling. At midnight, he hears the tap tap tap of the spiders' legs crawling up the window. He doesn't move, doesn't want to scare them away. He lifts his head an inch off his pillow to get a glimpse of them. Thousands of black hydraulic masterpieces swarm Bones' window. Sweet choir of the dark. They lift their voices, echo into the night. Night-night, Bones.

Bones is getting the best sleep of his life. He even dreams. He hasn't dreamed in so long, too long. Good for Bones. In fact, the sleep is so good that Bones never wants to wake up. Sleep forever. Dream forever. Goodnight, goodnight, goodnight. So he asks about moving in with them.

"Please, please, please," they say. "We've got all kinds of room for you."

"Can my friends visit me?" Bones asks.

"They might not like it," the spiders say.

"Will I like it?"

"Do you enjoy sleeping?"

Bones nods, tears up a little.

"Then you'll love it with us," they say.

Hooray! Bones is going away. He's off to live with spiders. So long!

Under blankets of moonlight they twirl on branches, in between dying leaves, spinning silk—blueprints to Bones' new home.

"Once you move in," they tell him, "we'll have dinner together every night, like a real family."

"I won't be hungry," he tells them.

"We will."

Bones doesn't even pack a bag. He just writes a note and tapes it to his front door in case anyone comes looking for him. It says: *Take what you want. I won't be back.*

The spiders tell Bones to meet them at the mouth of the woods down the street from his apartment. It opens like the pearly gates of heaven. They've built a kind of transportation thing from webbing for him. Bones sits down, rides through the trees and vines and dead things lying around. It's comfy as hell. 10/10 would recommend for travel.

"Relax. Lie back," they say.

Bones closes his eyes and listens as they take him through the blackness, umbrellaed by the thick pine above, suffocating what light may come from the moon and sky and stars, enveloping this new world in quiet mystery. He can sleep forever. Paradise. An eternal guest of Hotel Arachnid.

Their little legs are tapping. They're dancing a waltz or a jig or something. Probably a jig because it's speeding up and waltzes don't usually do that. His body sinks into the silk. It wraps around him tight like a blanket. Legs moving faster. They're crawling crawling crawling. Bones is drifting drifting drifting. Goodnight, Bones. Goodbye.

mtg minutes

EL SEGUNDO SECT OF THE SATANIC ASSEMBLY OF AMERICA (SAA)
Date: 8/10/2020 Start time: 6:00pm
Venue: Pasadena Hyatt Business Lobby

6:02pm — CALL TO ORDER/MINUTES
Last week's discussion topics:
- sacrificial offerings calendar
- upcoming election for council members and President
    * is mark of Satan still prerequisite for leadership?
    * ballot or blood?
    * drug tests — yes!
- congratulations to Wendell and Marcy on their new baby

6:17pm — FINANCE COMMITTEE UPDATE
Gains:
- post-bankruptcy Nic Cage movies
- Applebee's franchises (El Paso, Des Moines, Rancho Cucamonga, Boise)
Losses:
- NIN-themed weddings
- Applebee's franchises (Phoenix, Baton Rouge, Florida)

6:30pm — ENVIRONMENTAL AND SAFETY COMMITTEE UPDATES

- virus, fires, hurricanes, happy mistakes. Hail Satan!

6:44pm — DEBRIEF OF LAST MONTH'S MISSION TRIP TO ORANGE COUNTY

- white women prime candidates
- Target is a great place to evangelize
- Whole Foods also yielded great results
- apologies for the food poisoning (fish left out too long)
- group bonfire major success! (thanks Gil for providing the blankets)

7:15pm — lights in room explode

7:17pm — couch is on fire, room aglow in crimson

7:18pm — it's Keven (Satan's nephew)

7:22pm — President calls to order

7:25pm — Keven transforms into thirty-foot snake, eats two council members

(Note: While it is unknown whether or not Keven was aware, the two council members Keven ate were unable to apply for re-election as they have exceeded the allotted terms held by SAA members in accordance with bylaw X.23 Article V. No real harm done.)

7:32pm — President introduces the guest speaker for the evening, Keven

7:35pm — Keven takes the podium

- Keven sent by Satan to notify SAA of reorganization in Hell
- reorganization will affect current SAA members/committees
- SAA position titles will be reconfigured, rebranded
- SAA members must reapply for new positions in order to maintain membership
- applications will be open for 5 days internally, then 5 days externally
- election postponed until reorganization finalized

7:46pm — The council recognizes one of its members: "Hello, Roger Robinson, member since 1987. Lord Keven, can you explain the purpose of this reorganization? It seems abrupt. Also, will the number of positions within the SAA be consolidated or will there be somewhat of an expansion? Thank you."

7:47pm — Keven melts Roger's face off. Roger left screaming, begging for help on the floor. His body folds in half, sinks into the ground, down to Hell. Hail Satan!

7:52pm — "No more questions." - Keven

7:53pm — KEVEN PERFORMS CAKE'S "SATAN IS MY MO- TOR" WITH DEMON CHILD CHOIR

8:03pm — Keven turns into giant bat, flies out of the lobby and into the Hyatt Parking lot. Hotel guests screaming. Keven takes giant shit on frightened guests, flies through portal back to Hell. Hail Satan!

8:15pm — President motions to adjourn meeting

8:16pm — Gil seconds motion

8:16pm — All in favor? (all hands, aye)

8:17pm — Meeting adjourned. Hail Satan!

A Gallon of Water

The first time I got drunk, the first time I had a hangover, everyone told me to drink a gallon of water. They said I'd piss out all of the bad stuff and feel better and whatever. So I did and it worked. The first time I got high and had to take a drug test the next day, guess what I did. Ding ding, motherfucker. I drank another gallon. Passed with flying colors. I thought, maybe, possibly, this little trick might work for other shitty things too. When my girlfriend cheated on me with her sister's husband, I drank my one-hundred and twenty-eight ounces. Pissed like a firehose. All was forgiven. She left me a few months later for her old high school English teacher. I drank, I pissed, I moved on. Bye, babe. Don't think twice and all that. I bought one of those gallon-sized plastic water bottles you see all those hard-nippled bodybuilders carrying around at the gym or at GNC, kept it with me all the time. At my mother's funeral. When my dad said he'd wished it was my funeral. After getting fired from Guitar Center. Losing my health insurance. When I got arrested for spray painting dicks on that school bus. Getting kicked out of my aunt's place. Trying and failing to get my GED. When someone stole my identity. Watching the girl I love marry that guy I hate. Getting my car repossessed. Drink, drink, drink. Piss, piss, piss. I never felt better. King of the world! No, king of the galaxy! King of kings!

At some point, and I can't remember when, I stopped pissing altogether. I thought, maybe my body had gotten used to being so hydrated. Maybe I just needed to step up my game, drink more water to flush out the water that was still stuck inside, taking up the space that all of the bad thoughts and bad feelings might otherwise occupy. I drank another gallon. Nothing. Another. Nada. Gallon after gallon after gallon. I drank from the faucet, from the hose, from the fire hydrant, from the sewer, from the toilet, from the lakes and rivers and mountains springs.

It started in my pinky fingers, spread to my ring finger, middle finger, and so on. My hands blew up like balloons. Then my toes, my feet, legs. Another gallon is probably all I need, right? And another. And another. And another. And one more. Not an ounce of piss left my body. I took a safety pin, tried stabbing it into my forearm. I grabbed a razor, a knife, a saw. Nothing penetrated my skin. Like goddamn steel.

For days there was just stretching, stretching, stretching. My limbs wouldn't bend, wouldn't budge. I could hear the water sloshing around inside my organs. Eventually, my weight cracked the cement I was standing on. The sidewalk widened its mouth as I sank. I went down, down, down. I couldn't see anything or hear anything. Total fucking darkness. I felt nothing as dirt and rock scraped by.

I thought about all those things I'd avoided, all the things I'd never felt. I wanted to be depressed, manic, suicidal, bitter, lost, helpless, anxious, insane, empty, dead inside. A whole world of miserable people trampled above, free and fleeting in their perpetual self-loathing. O, to anguish! To hate myself! To hate others! To hate all creation! Glorious, wonderful misery!

At the earth's core, everyone and everything that had ever existed sat in fold-out chairs, waiting for their number to be called so they could walk into the fire and disappear forever.

I wondered, when it's finally my turn, if the countless gallons I'd swallowed would put out the flame or if I would be afforded any kind of suffering at all.

Good Luck With Your Dog

My therapist tells me to go on a bicycle tour. "It's great exercise," she says, "and it'll be good for you to actually get out of the house, where it happened, and see the world a little bit." Bless her, she's trying her best but nothing seems to take away the pain since Elroy, my dog, died. Well, technically, he didn't die, he disappeared. No, disappeared isn't the right word for it, either. It's not like he ran away or anything. We were watching television and he heard something outside I guess, but when he jumped off the couch to see what it was, he got sucked through an invisible wormhole or something. I ran after him, but the wormhole was gone. All I can think of now is poor Elroy running for his life from some dog-eating creature on another plane of existence. The science professors at the community college near me say, sometimes it happens, get a new dog. I go to therapy instead.

I'm not able to find any cycling groups on Craigslist or Facebook or the community board at the library. There're a few ads for spin classes, but my therapist said a tour not a class. As I'm walking out of the bike shop with a new tube for my rear tire, this guy with those horn implants in his head comes up to me and says, "What kinda bike you got?"

"An old Bianchi. But it's in good condition. It was my dad's."

"Fuck your dad. Wanna ride with us?"

I look around, he's alone.

"Yes or no?"

"Yeah, alright. When and where?"

He tells me to meet him behind the old Presbyterian church a few miles outside of town and to bring a backpack with food and water and maybe a jacket or sweater.

"Cool. I like your horns," I say.

He ignores me, walks into the store.

About fifteen people or so are waiting behind the church when I get there. It's over ninety degrees and the humidity is high so I'm already sweating like crazy. Everyone else is wearing black onesies and their faces are covered in tattoos. One of them smiles at me, sticks out his tongue. It's forked. I give a thumbs up because what the fuck do I do with that? There's one other person there who looks lost like me. She walks up and introduces herself. Her name is Jandy. She says it's her first ride with this group. I say, me too. The dude with the horns rides up. His handlebars are shaped to look like horns. This guy is really into horns.

Horn guy calls us over, makes us stand in a circle. He says if we're new to the group, don't introduce yourself, no one cares. Just follow him and do what he says and don't veer away from the group or it's your ass, not his. Jandy and I look at each other like, shit, but it's too late now I guess. I'm in this, I need this. For Elroy. Poor Elroy. Horn guy's wide eyes work their way around the circle, locking with everyone else's as he prays:

Take us into your belly.

Let us be guided by the chaos of your darkness.

We offer ourselves up as sacrifices, blood and flesh and pain. We fear you.

He smiles, spits on the ground. "Let's ride, fuckers," he says.

There's a narrow entrance that leads beneath the church, leading to some underground road below, a tunnel or something. The walls are crumbling brick. Graffiti everywhere, drawings of dicks and 666 and, I think, Godzilla. It smells like piss and stale bread and rubbing alcohol. It reminds me of Chuck E. Cheese. There are Christmas lights strung up that seem to go on forever, into pinpoint blackness. The guy with the forked tongue coasts by, flicks his tongue at me. "Better keep up," he says. Another thumbs up.

Jandy rolls up next to me and asks how I ended up on this ride. I tell her about Elroy. She says she's not surprised, there's been a rise in sporadic wormholes across the state. The media won't cover it. Too dangerous. I don't ask her for her story but she tells me anyway. She's looking for the detached wings of fallen angels. Says they make your skin pretty and make you fertile and they're worth a shit ton of money on the black market. She heard from a friend of a friend of a friend of a friend that these guys know where to find some, so she tracked them down and here she is. "Anyways," she says, "good luck with your dead dog!"

My legs start cramping when we hit a slope that takes us further down. I don't have to pedal for at least five minutes. We just keep going down, down, down further and further and weeeeee this is actually sorta fun! But I start to wonder what my therapist would think because, really, I'm not exactly seeing the world. I'm not seeing much of anything except the Christmas lights and brick walls that are, wait, oozing? Yeah, they're oozing something. I think maybe we're under a river or lake but it's not coming out like water it's coming out like that pink shit on Ghostbusters II. The kind that Ray and Winston and Egon had to swim through two-thirds of the way through the movie.

Horn guy yells back at us, "Watch your shit!"

There's something moving ahead, like a shadow of a shadow. The shadow of a shadow starts speaking in a language that is probably Latin or something because isn't everything that's kinda scary somehow spoken in Latin? Horn guy screams, "Yes, Lord!" I watch him rise in the air, still pedaling, drifting toward the shadow of a shadow. He's laughing. He's so happy. Good for him. The shadow of a shadow opens its mouth, its teeth like boulders, crunches down on Horn guy. Some of the group hoots and hollers while others scream we're all gonna die! we're all gonna die! we're all gonna die! I lift my ass off my seat and pedal as hard and as fast as I can, wishing my therapist could see me now.

The bricks in the walls are falling out and the ooze is gushing out. It slops on the floor, makes a few of the other riders skid out and crash. But they don't really crash per se. They sort of… melt into the ooze. Limbs sizzle and smoke, sinking into the thick slime.

A few riders fly by me, frantic. Then, all the blackness disappears and the tunnel is illuminated by mountains of fire up ahead. The brick walls have all crumbled. At our sides is the black ooze steaming. Above the ooze, winged creatures are flying around, screeching and throwing spears at the riders. They nail a few riders and swoop down to pick them up and fly off with them. They leave the bikes.

It's just me, Jandy, and the guy with the forked tongue now. The guy with the forked tongue keeps switching between laughing and crying but he makes the same face for both so it's sorta funny but also sad. Up ahead there's another tunnel, leading into further blackness. Right before we dip, the guy with the forked tongue screams. I look back to watch him being ripped in half, vertically, by two shadow of a shadow monsters. Should've kept up.

This tunnel looks like the one we first went into: graffiti, brick walls, Chuck E. Cheese smell. It's colder, though. Like, really fucking cold. Jandy and I slow down. My legs are turning into icicles.

"We're not gonna make it," Jandy says.

I think about Elroy. He'd want me to push through. Dig deep. Carry on. Go! Fight! Win!

We inch along. Ice stretching across our arms, back, chest. We inch for hours, not sure how far we've gone.

Then, a light ahead. Daylight. Sunshine. Earth. Our legs find their strength. We pedal faster, harder. Green grass and blue skies within eyeshot. My legs move at super speed. I'm the Flash. I'm Superman. I'm Lance fucking Armstrong. We shoot out of the tunnel entrance, our tires on fire. I jump from my bike, watch it fly off into the woods. I turn, see the church behind me. We're back where we started. Jandy stands beside her bike, drinking her bottled water, eating a Zero bar.

"I'm sorry you didn't find your wings," I say.

"It's fine. Maybe they're somewhere else."

"Maybe."

"Do you feel better about your dead…"

I'm pulled at the waist. The world expands. Noiseless. Grey. I'm a noodle.

Elroy sits next to me on the couch, watching the weather. He looks up and stares at me.

Better Than Dead: Forgotten

Some families are the kind of families that are made of rainbows and sunshine and some are made of a good economy and savvy business investments. Mine was the kind of family that if you got too close, even just a little, your brain would calcify or your insides would liquify or you'd just go BOOM! You know the kind. It was a bad situation. Real bad. The worst, actually. All my life it was one catastrophic event after another: the icecaps melted and we all drowned while sitting at the kitchen table, snakes nested under our beds and attacked us while we slept, one of us got boils so all of us got boils. Like I said, the worst. So, when my family kicked me out of the family, it wasn't really the end of the world. Of course, if you ask them, they'll say it was mostly all my fault. They'll say I was the problem. They'll say I was always causing trouble in one way or another. They'll say lots of things. Family's funny that way, I guess. Except, it's not so much funny ha-ha as it is funny like I should have turned into a real asshole or whatever but it's fine, I'm totally fine, everything is a-okay. See?

After I left my family's home, I set out into the wilderness to fend for myself. It was easy-peasy in the beginning. I ate the mushrooms and the berries and the apples and cucumbers and French dip sandwiches that grew on the trees. I found a great cave that came fully furnished with a recliner and a television and a small library with books by Zac Smith and Bud Smith and mainly authors with the last name Smith. That was just fine by me. I like those guys. Good stuff. A+. 10/10. I stayed there for a few years. I read all the books and watched all the shows on the television and took all the naps and it was really cool. Very fun. I got into making my own beer and sold six-packs to the other cave-dwellers. I donated all the proceeds to a local orphanage because I felt like, in a way, I was an orphan. But I wouldn't let myself dwell on that feeling because I dwelled in a cave and not in misery. Amirite? LOL! Whenever I'd feel sad or angry or like I wanted to bash my head against my living room rock, I'd drink my beer until I couldn't stand up straight and I'd just fall asleep. See? No more sad times. Besides, the other cave-dwellers who came to buy my beer and drink my beer were sort of like my makeshift family, anyway. I could live with that. I mean, at that point, I'd have taken anything over my real family. At least this makeshift version of a family didn't set my feet on fire or pull my fingernails out when they thought I was happier than they were. At least there was that. At least.

When the winds came, they blew all of us cave-dwellers out of the wilderness and into the city where there weren't any fully furnished places to live or books by authors named Smith or French dip sand-wiches that didn't cost $16.99 and taste like wet farts. We were scattered along the sidewalks and under the bus stop benches and on top of liquor stores and laundromats. Now that I was back in the city and had cell service again, all the text messages my family had sent me while I was in the caves went ding ding ding on my phone for a really long time.

Mom: I am *still* your mother!

Dad: Are you mad at me?

Brother: ARRGGUUUGGHHH!!!!

Sister: wya?

The best thing I could do for myself at that point was block, un-follow, unfriend, goodbye! I took the last of the beer I made and drank it on top of a freeway advertisement saying that Jesus was coming back so get your shit together, man, or something like that. I felt sad but I felt free and that was weird but oh well life goes on, right? Sure. Okay.

I liked living on top of the Jesus advertisement. The city looked like a pinball machine with lights bouncing around the buildings. From the sign you couldn't smell the piss on the sidewalk. It smelled like fresh rain. It was quiet and I could keep to myself, and I mostly kept to myself until the morning I woke up and found Alice sleeping a few feet away. Her hair had all kinds of leaves that reminded me of fall in it and her clothes were tattered in a way that reminded me of Seattle.

"Hi. Hello." I told her.

She smiled, waved at me. "Hi. Hello."

"I live here."

"It's very nice here."

"Thank you. Why are you here?"

"I saw you in the caves. I used to live there, too. Your beer was great. I never cared for beer before, but yours was great. I like beer now."

"Thanks."

"You're welcome. Anyway, I've been living in the sewer for the past few weeks but got chased out last night by the scuba diving squad." She took an orange leaf from her hair and rolled it up, blew it out into the world. "I saw you up here but couldn't ask if it was okay if I spend the night because you were asleep. So, I came up anyway. Better to ask for forgiveness than not to bother in the first place."

Alice and I got married a few months later under the overpass near our Jesus sign home. Everyone from the wilderness and the caves came to celebrate us. They brought honey and ferns and papier-mâché sculptures and blueberry pies and alligator teeth necklaces and more and more and more and more. After we said we do and kissed and gave each other tattoos they carried us on a float through the downtown portion of the city. I don't remember how the people in the city reacted because I was too busy watching Alice catch leaves in her hair and the shapes she made with the leaves and how when she blew them back into the universe everything felt fresh and alive.

Our first baby died. That part of the story stays with me. I'm sorry.

When our daughter turned eight and our son turned six, we took them to the wilderness. We showed them the cave where Alice lived with her family. We showed them the cave where I lived with the books.

Our daughter asked, "Dad, where's your family?"

"You're my family," I said.

Our son asked, "Are they dead?"

"Better than dead: forgotten," I said.

"Cool," he said.

Our daughter took berries and ground them up and wrote our family name on the tree in front of the entrance to the wilderness. The entrance I walked through after my ex-family kicked me out of their family. Our son sharpened a rock and carved our family name in the spot where our daughter had written our family name in the tree to the entrance of the wilderness that I walked through after my ex-family kicked me out of their family. I wanted to cry but I didn't only because they were so happy and even though I was so happy I didn't want them thinking I was sad because I wasn't. Emotions are confusing like that sometimes.

After we got home to our newly renovated Scientology sign that used to be the Jesus sign, we tucked the kids into bed and sat out front.

"Hi. Hello. I love you," Alice said.

I watched the tapestry of headlights on the freeway and the meteorites flying overhead. I listened to the orchestra of pint glasses filled with the beer I'd been making with new ingredients going cling clang cling clang throughout the city below.

"Hi. Hello. I love you," I said.

Clouds

I tell Arnie that Shelley broke up with me again. This time, I think she means it, I say. This time, I guess I messed up pretty bad. This time, I tried to kill her dad. And I only did it because that's what I thought she wanted me to do. She was like, God, I wish someone'd just kill him already. So, I got the hammer and I got the plastic and found a field and dug a hole and there you have it. Wham! Bam! See ya later, alligator! I tell him how she walked in on me right before I brought the hammer down on the back of his head. Right before it was lights out for him. Right before I could whisk her off into the sunset and into forever and into always and all that. She said she was only joking when she said she wished someone'd just kill her dad. She said she didn't actually want him dead. She said she only said that because she was angry and that I never should've taken her seriously. She said I have issues, a lot of issues. She said it's over. She said goodbye forever, see ya later alligator!

Arnie stares at the clouds, sees through the clouds, scrutinizes what's on the other side of the clouds. I look up at the clouds. Nothing there but clouds. Just bulbous smoke monsters morphing into silhouettes of me and Shelley laughing and happy and together like nothing bad ever happened, like I didn't try to kill her dad. I start to cry, then Arnie pats my back because he's a good friend, I guess.

He asks if I still have the hammer and the plastic and the field I found with the hole I dug.

I say yes.

He says he has an idea and that it wasn't all for nothing if you ask him.

I don't ask him, but okay.

Sometimes, he says, when one door closes, there's a whole bunch of other doors so just fucking pick one, you know?

I say okay.

The inside of Arnie's garage is like a junkyard for old appliances. It's full of old computers and old car batteries and old Christmas lights and extension cords and microwaves and washing machines and stoplights and cell phones and CD players and televisions. You pretty much name it, he's got it. I sit down on one of those electric shopping carts you find at grocery stores for people who can't walk and people who don't want to walk while Arnie tosses everything around the garage.

I ask, what are you up to?

He says, you'll see.

I say, okay.

He asks, do you have anywhere to be?

I shake my head no.

He says to just chill, hang out, relax a bit while he goes to work on something he thinks will make me feel a lot better. It's something he's been wanting to try for a while, he says.

I say okay.

He drags a metal box out of the corner that's about six feet long and three feet wide and is covered by a blue tarp and goes skreeeeek skreeeeek as he drags it across the concrete. After Arnie muscles it to the center of the garage, he removes the blue tarp. Arnie's smile reminds me of that movie *Critters* even though Arnie is much better looking than the critters in *Critters*. This is it, he says. This is your ticket!

I ask what is it?

He tells me it's a time machine. He says it works, but it only takes you back a couple of days. He says I can use it to go back in time and stop myself from killing Shelley's dad.

I ask how do I do that?

He says, you gotta kill yourself, dude. Kill yourself and start over, he says. If you go back in time before you try to kill Shelley's dad and kill yourself instead and bury yourself in the hole you dug, she won't break up with you and she won't think you have real bad issues and it'll all be okay.

I say okay.

Arnie gives me a high-five before he locks me in the time machine and sends me into the past. He hands me my hammer and my giant roll of plastic. He tells me to close my eyes. He says cover my nuts, too. He says he'll see me in a couple of days ago.

I say okay.

The door to the time machine box closes, and I close my eyes and cover my nuts and hear a whoosh and a bzzzz. Everything goes quiet and the door unlocks. I open it and I'm alone in Arnie's garage, under the blue tarp, tucked away in the corner. It's dark and the moonlight drips through the window and onto the garage walls and onto the cement floor. Arnie isn't here. I trip over a few wires and a coffee maker before I sneak out and try to track my past self down.

I find me in the field, digging the hole and sweating a lot more than I remember. I should work out more. My past self doesn't hear me sneak up behind him. Just as he stomps the shovel into the dirt, I smack my hammer on the back of his head. Blood pours from his head, my head, black and thick and ew ew ew. I push him into the hole. I shovel the dirt onto his limp body. I keep watch over my shoulder to make sure no one catches me attempting to cover up my self-murder/suicide. I feel myself sweating the way I saw myself sweating a few moments ago before I killed myself.

R.I.P. me.

I get home and take a shower, fall asleep on my couch. I dream of the cumulus clouds shifting and reconstructing themselves into images of me smashing the hammer down on my own head, of Arnie electrocuting himself with jumper cables and an oven, of Shelley and her dad waving at me as they get into the time machine box — see ya later, alligator!

When I wake up, I get dressed, head to Shelley's. She's on her front porch, smoking a cigarette and sweating like I was sweating when I dug that hole. She jumps when she sees me.

I ask, are you okay?

She says she did something bad. Something really, really bad, she says.

I tell her I'm here now. I tell her everything is going to be okay.

I killed my dad, she says.

I ask her why she killed her dad.

She says, I didn't know what else to do. She says she didn't think I'd have taken her seriously if she'd asked me outright to do it. She said she'd hoped I'd had gotten the hint the other day, but she didn't think I did.

I leave Shelley, drive home. On the ride back, I think about killing myself. I think about my sad, sweaty, rotting body in the hole I dug in the field I found. I think about Arnie and his time machine and the clouds and all the different doors Arnie was telling me about. I walk through my door. Something goes crack and everything goes dark.

Arnie says, this is fucking amazing! this is fucking amazing!

Someone says to Arnie, he tried to kill me! he tried to kill me!

I open my eyes and see Arnie and me standing a few feet away, staring wide-eyed and manic like the critters in *Critters*. I can't move. I'm tied to a chair. My head hurts real bad.

Arnie is holding a hammer, the same hammer I used to kill myself last night, a few days ago. The me I thought I killed is slumped against the wall with a bag of ice taped to the back of his head and dried blood on his face and dirt all over his clothes.

It didn't work, I say.

What didn't work, Arnie asks.

The other me says, shut the fuck up. He takes the hammer from Arnie's hand and raises it like he's going to smack it on the front of my skull the way I smacked it on the back of his skull. Arnie pulls the hammer from nearly-dead me's hand and tells him to fucking chill. He asks me again what didn't work.

I tell him about Shelley breaking up with me and I tell him about the time machine and about his idea for me to kill myself and how something went wrong and now I have to figure out a way to go back to a few days from now but I don't know how and will he please untie me.

Everyone stays quiet for a while. I look at me, he looks at Arnie, Arnie looks at the time machine.

Arnie says he has an idea. He walks toward the time machine but before he can pull off the blue tarp the box door flies off and crashes against the wall and every version of me from every possible universe pours out of the time machine the way the blood poured from my head when I tried to kill myself with the hammer in the field last night a few days ago. There's an old me with metal legs. There's a me carrying Shelley's head on a stick. There's a me that's a werewolf. There's a me that's green. A me that's translucent. A me that's the female version of me. All the mes that ever me-ed.

First, they kill the me that I didn't fully kill. They take their hammers and bash in his skull until his head looks like a bowl of soup. Then, they wrap Arnie in their plastic wrap and set him on fire. I hear him screaming and gurgling and crying and oh my god oh my god oh my god! As more versions of me pour out of the time machine, they turn on one another, maiming one another, killing one another, slaughtering one another. They pick me up, keeping me tied to the chair, and lock me inside the time machine. From inside I hear the skreeeeek skreeeeeek as they drag the time machine across the garage. The skreeeeeks turn into krrrnnnnkkkkk as they drag it outside into Archie's backyard.

One of me says, cover your eyes and your nuts!

The female version of me says, he can't, dumbass! He's tied up.

The time machine goes whoosh whoosh whoosh whoosh bzzzz bzzz bzzz bzzzz and sparks fly and the blackness in front of me begins to spark and gravity dissipates.

Light the size of a pinpoint expands until a blue sky opens above me and cumulus clouds form around me and morph into Shelley smiling at me as I hurl down down down — see ya later, alligator!

Puzzles

For months, I've been making my own puzzles. It's real easy. Lots of fun. Good times. I start by taking old pictures of family or friends or loved ones or ex-girlfriends or dead pets and tear the pictures into a thousand pieces of various sizes and shapes. Then, I get hammered, crank the record player to full volume and dance like nobody's watching or like everybody's watching. I don't even care. La-de-dah! After blacking the fuck out, I hide the pieces all over my apartment: behind bookshelves, under the sink, in mouseholes, under the floor, in the ceiling, down the toilet, in the mattress, etc. etc. etc.

The next morning I'll wake up with a serious hangover or a voice-mail from my boss telling me I'm fired or blah blah blah but whatever, man, this is my favorite game. After I sober up, I try to find where I hid the pieces, try putting them back together. Let's go! At first, I got real frustrated and gave up a lot or put the wrong pieces together and ended up with something like a mutation of my cousin, Tyler, and my dog, Carl. But I kept at it and got good. Like, really good. Like, you'd be super impressed by how good I am. Aren't you proud of me?

The pictures get to be too easy, so I try hiding user guides for appliances or instruction manuals for putting furniture together: Whirlpool washing machines and IKEA dressers and HP wireless printers. I sneak into my neighbors' apartments while they sleep and hide pieces to make it harder on myself. One time a neighbor catches me in her kitchen, hiding pieces of a Roomba warranty card. She comes out brandishing a crowbar, asks me what I'm doing, who I am, yada yada yada. I must've hidden her because I haven't seen her since then and I haven't bothered to find her either. Whoops! My bad.

When you're super good and stuff like I am, you have to find new ways to challenge yourself. I decide to up the stakes of the hide and seek puzzles game I play with myself. Instead of using photos or paper or paintings, I start cutting off pieces of my body. A finger here. A toe there. You get it. I use a phone book and choose addresses at random to send my severed appendages. I'm drinking more often, drunk more frequently, completely blitzed most of the time. My liver hurts. My liver can get the fuck over it. Between that and the bleeding and the passing out and LMAO! Most of the time, I find my fingers and toes and ear lobes and such after a few days of riding the bus, blood spewing all over, asking patrons if they've seen whatever body part I'm looking for, telling them no no no, I'm fine, no hospital needed, it's a game, chill. Anyway, I'd find my body parts, take them home, sew myself up, and there I am—good as new!

Look, the last thing I want to be accused of is being a braggart, but I have to admit that I'm scaring myself by how good I am at this. So, I'm going for broke. Put up or shut up. Go big or go home. Do or die, baby! Woohoo!

This morning, I took a kitchen knife and dug it into my chest and worked my way past my ribcage and my lungs and cut out my heart. I hear a phantom heartbeat, but I know it's not there. I know I've hidden it somewhere far away, somewhere it'll likely take me a long time to find. And I will find it. Oh yeah, I will. As soon as I can get back up. As soon as I regain feeling in my legs. As soon as the ceiling stops spinning. As soon as it warms up just a bit. You just wait. I'll find it. I'm good at this game. Really good. You'll see. Yeah, you'll see.

Makeover

After he loses his job and his wife fakes her death and leaves him for her boss and his kids disown him and his house burns down and his identity is stolen and his health insurance expires and his prescription runs out and his cat runs away and his dog kills itself and his transmission goes clank clank kaput and he gets gout in his foot and his mother and his father die on a Carnival Cruise and his credit score drops to zero and his college revokes his degree and on and on and on and on and on, Dirk nominates himself to get a makeover by a couple of super famous makeover specialists he'd seen on television before his television was stolen, before his house burned to the ground. Ashes to ashes. Poof!

Dirk waits for the makeover specialists in the parking lot of Lowe's. He watches one of those giant inflatable air dancers at the car dealership across the street dance up and down and side to side and woooo look at it go!

The makeover specialists show up an hour and forty-five minutes late. They ride in on motorcycles shaped like stags that shoot massive flames out of their asses whenever they rev the engine. Super badass.

"We would have been here sooner but we thought we saw a wormhole and when we pulled over to examine what we thought was a wormhole we discovered it was absolutely nothing at all," they tell Dirk.

"Shit. Bummer," Dirk says.

"We're still very disappointed," they say.

"Yeah."

They ask Dirk to show them where he lives. They want to see everything that's still a part of his life, still a part of his existence, everything he's holding on to, everything he has a hard time letting go of. All of it. Leave no stone unturned and all that shit, you know? This is very important, they say. Don't lie, don't hide.

He tells them he's been sleeping in a shed behind a Western Union. He tells them that the Western Union manager doesn't mind him staying there so long as he doesn't make a lot of noise or scare off any customers whenever the manager actually gets customers.

A single lightbulb sways back and forth bringing only a little light into the 10'x12' room. Little bits of mouse shit are scattered on the shelves. Rusty tools hang on the wall. A pile of brick, the bottom layer crumbling, in the corner. A wooden stool and a blow-up mattress, no sheets, no pillow, take up the rest of the space.

The two makeover specialists look the room over, look Dirk over. "We're getting rid of all this baggage," they say.

The first makeover specialist takes out a bag that may or may not have been made with human skin and sifts through the bag until they pull out a pair of pliers.

"Open wide," they say.

Dirk leans his head back and opens his mouth so wide his jaw almost comes unhinged.

The second makeover specialist holds a flashlight over Dirk's face while the first makeover specialist removes each of Dirk's teeth one by one.

"These are holding you back," they say.

Dirk stays still, swallowing his blood and saliva.

After Dirk's teeth are removed, they tell Dirk to undress. "Nudity. Let's see it," they say.

Dirk strips bare. His chest and back and legs and shoulders and ass and balls are covered with hair. It's impossible to see his skin. It's hard to tell whether he even has skin. For all the makeover specialists know, he is made predominantly of hair.

The first makeover specialist goes back to the bag that may or may not be made of human skin and pulls out two long black ponchos and hands one to the second makeover specialist.

Dirk tries saying something, but blood just spills from the holes in his mouth.

They ignore him. "Turn around and close your eyes," they say.

Dirk does.

"You can turn around now."

Dust and gnats flit across the ceiling and under the single light bulb keeping the shed from complete darkness. The two makeover specialists remove their clothes and put on long black ponchos. The first makeover specialist holds a skinning knife. The second makeover specialist holds a bucket.

"Stay still," they say. They shave Dirk's hair down until only his flaky skin is visible. "This isn't working," they say.

They start removing his skin in large patches.

Dirk goes in and out of consciousness. The light warbling around him, the sound of his flesh going squish squish, a growing disconnectedness.

They slop each stretch of skin in the bucket until the bucket is overflowing with pieces of Dirk.

"How do you feel?"

Dirk smiles, the muscles in his face exposed.

They cut out his muscle tissue. "No," they say.

They sever each nerve ending one by one. "No."

They disconnect his bones. "No."

They remove his small organs. "Nope."

They take his brain and heart and lungs and put them in trash bags. "No no no. Goodbye!"

Dirk's soul hangs in the air, floating next to the single lightbulb that swings back and forth in the middle of the room. Dirk watches as the two makeover specialists take his remains outside and burn them in a trash can.

The two makeover specialists come back in the shed and examine Dirk's soul, tears in their eyes. "This is our best work. The greatest thing we've ever done for anyone. You deserve this, honey. You're beautiful. You're amazing. You dazzle. You light up the room. You're magnificently remarkably irrevocably fucking perfect! You are anything and everything you want to be."

At first, he feels nothing. He waits. He continues to feel nothing. No emotion whatsoever. He thinks that this should scare the shit out of him but meh. Nope. Nothing. Nada. Zip. Zilich. Wait, did he just… Nope, still nothing, ha! Wowee! What a feeling to feel nothing at all! To not give a shit who his wife is fucking, where his kids are, what he should add to update his LinkedIn profile, if he should brush up on his coding skills, what bills are still unpaid, his credit score, why he's pissing blood, where we go when we die, who to vote for, cholesterol, recession, global warming, sadism, narcissism, the expanding universe, the book of Revelation, heat stroke, social justice, and on and on and on and on and on and on.

Dirk floats freely, elegantly, like a symphony, like a summer breeze, like an air dancer at a car dealership. Wooo, look at him go!

Big Day Off

My boss calls, says he needs me to come in today. Says there's a big project that needs to get done today. Not tomorrow. Not next week. Today. No one else can do it, he says. No one else has the talent, the skill, the grit, the goddamn ingenuity. A lot is riding on this project, he says. It's gotta be me.

No can do, I tell him. Super sorry. Today's my day off. Big plans for today.

We really need you, he says. The company will fail if you don't help, he says.

Sounds rough, I say. You'll figure it out. Good luck! Click.

My girlfriend calls, wants to know if she can come over. Wants to know if I'd like to spend some quality time together. Says she'll cook for me. Rub my back. Feed me grapes and meats and crackers and cheese. Says she'll bring a bottle or six of wine and we can get drunk and fuck and I can do that one thing I've been wanting to do but she's been too hesitant. Says today's the day she wants to try new things. Yippee!

Sorry, babe. Gotta take a rain check. Click.

My landlord calls, says he wants to give me the deed to my building. You've been a wonderful tenant, he says. The best ever. I'm also giving you all your rent back. You earned it.

Thank you! Thank you! Thank you!

I just need you to come down and sign the paperwork today, he says. Before the bank closes, he says.

Bummer. Call me tomorrow, I say. Click.

The mayor calls. Well, her secretary calls, technically. The mayor would like to talk to you, she says.

I'm busy, I say.

The mayor gets on the line. I'm awarding you the key to the city, she says. You're a great human. A wonderful man. Pillar of our community. Etc.

Cool, thanks.

We're hosting a ceremony for you right now. How soon can you be here?

Tomorrow, I say.

It needs to be today, she tells me. Or else we've got to give the key to someone else.

Yes ma'am. I understand. Do what you have to do. Thanks. Click.

A representative for a major motion picture company calls. They've read my stories. They love them all. Every single one. Like, literally, OMG, all of them. They want to sign me for all kinds of deals: movies, television shows, Netflix series. Big directors! Big actors! Big money! Big, baby, big! They've booked a ticket to Hollywood for me.

Wow! Whoa! Amazing! Incredible!

Your flight leaves this afternoon, they say.

Sorry, Tinseltown. Can't make it today. Click.

God calls, says he's giving it all up. He's going on permanent vacation, getting out of town, starting fresh. He says he wants to hand it all over to me. You'll be in charge, he says. The big guy, he says. The dude upstairs, he says. You can do better than me, he tells me. He says I'm the only one he trusts to run all of creation. He just needs go over a few operational things with me before he exits existence tonight.

Click.

My dog sits in front of me, looks up with his big brown eyes.

You ready?

We drive to the lake. I throw his rope. He brings it back. I throw it again. We eat ham sandwiches and drink beer and walk around the water. We sit on a blanket and watch the sun set golden behind a skyline of shimmering buildings. He puts his head on my lap and I rub his ears until he falls asleep.

Click.

Clark

I get into a really bad accident. I'm riding in a shopping cart that's attached to the back of my buddy's truck and my buddy sees a deer and swerves, but I don't swerve because shopping carts don't have decent brakes or steering wheels. I go weeeeeeeeeeeeeeeee off a fifty-foot drop and then go boom-crash at the bottom. My brain farts out and I die. Being dead is a lot like waiting at the DMV except the tellers aren't mean assholes, they're cute little dogs and cats. That way, when they tell you you're not getting into heaven, you're like, awwwww ok, cutie pie! But, yeah, anyway, totally dead. Oh, fuck! Oh, no! It's cool, though. The doctors bring me back to life after a few hours or maybe days. I don't know exactly how long I'm dead for, tbh. But look! See? I'm all shiny and new. Yay!

When I wake up from being dead and stuff, the doctors and the nurses and hospital janitors are all standing around the room laughing and high-fiving and taking shots and having sex with one another because they brought me back to life like Jesus and that Lazarus guy. While they're all celebrating, I see this guy floating above me as I'm lying on my hospital bed. It's obvious, right? He's a ghost. Bingo!

I point at him, ask anyone who can hear me, "Who's that?"

No one else seems to notice him.

"You need to rest," a nurse says.

"Hi there! I'm Clark," Clark says to only me because no one else can see him.

"It's probably a side effect from being dead," the doctor tells me. "It'll wear off over time."

Do you remember those My Buddy dolls? You know those dolls that you carried around as a little kid and the jingle went something like *My buddy, my buddy, wherever I go, you're gonna go! My Buddy! My buddy and me!* Clark sort of becomes like the ghost version of My Buddy because he's always there wherever I go no matter what. It takes some time, but I get used to it. I like to think of Clark as, like, the holy spirit or something. Except Clark wears a yellow polo shirt and green sweatpants and has a ponytail. I don't know what the holy spirit looks like, but I don't think it looks like Clark.

Clark tells me he's not haunting me on purpose or anything. That he should be on the other side but for some reason he's stuck with me. Every time he tries to leave, he ends up right back here with me.

"I'm sorry if I'm bothering you," he says.

"Not at all, my dude."

I like having Clark around.

Clark and I are sitting on the roof of an old, abandoned movie theater. I'm on my fifth beer. Clark's chilling, relaxing. It's Tuesday. We see these girls running across the street, yelling and laughing and having the time of their lives. One of them spots us on the roof, sees me crack open another Modelo.

She yells, "Hey! You got any more beer?"

"I got some more beer," I holler back.

"I like your ponytail," the other one says to Clark. "I'm Kat."

Clark and I lose our shit. See, no one else but me has ever seen Clark. So, it seems appropriate for us to lose our shit.

Clark goes, "You can see me?"

The girls go, "Yeah. Can you see us?"

The girls make it to the roof of the movie theater, each take a beer from the pack, cheers, and chug the cans down. I think I'm in love. We sit in a circle, stare at each other.

"I'm Clark," Clark says. "I'm a ghost."

"I'm Kat. She's Irene. That's cool," Kat says.

I say, "Yeah, it's cool."

Irene tells us that they're psychics. That's how they can see Clark.

Clark says that's neat.

Kat asks Clark how long he's been a ghost.

"I don't know. I can't remember exactly. I don't think it's been that long to be honest. I mean, I remember killing myself, and that doesn't seem too long ago."

That's news to me. I've never asked Clark how he died, so that's my bad. But still. Sorta heavy, you know? "Is that why you didn't go to the afterlife DMV? Because you'd go to hell?"

Clark says, "No. I just never went." He goes on to tell us that after he killed himself he just sort of showed up in my hospital room, watching the doctors and nurses party it up because I wasn't dead anymore. He never went to the DMV like me. He thinks that's kind of manipulative, but he gets it, he says. Puppies and kittens would make the transition to hell easier.

"Well, I'm glad you're here with us," Irene says.

An hour later me and the girls are drunk, dancing and throwing our beer cans off the roof. Clark isn't saying much. He's got a look on his face like he doesn't mind being there but if he had a choice, he'd rather be anywhere else. I wonder if he's upset that we're alive and having a good time and he's not or if he's upset because he's dead and we're not.

I ask Clark what he wants to do. I ask if there's anything that he did when he was alive that he'd like to do even though he's not anymore. Maybe it'll be different and more fun now that he's dead.

"Nah, I killed myself for a reason," he says.

"For sure. For sure."

"You have unfinished business, Clark," Kat says, running her hand over Clark's translucent hand.

Clark bursts into little ghost tears. Ghost snot running down his ghost nose. His essence shakes, goes staticky. It gets cold, like the season changed. Winter is here. We turn into ice cubes. Frozen in sadness. Brrrr. Boohoo. I think for sure I'm going back to the afterlife DMV.

Sort of looking forward to seeing all those cute little pups telling me that eternal damnation is waiting for me behind door number two.

"I never got to say goodbye," Clark says, choking on a sob.

"To who?"

"She was the love of my life, man. Her name was Sarah. We were best friends as kids and fell in love when we got older. But shit happened and, I don't know, we just sort of lost contact, you know? Everything felt right with her. Like, when you go to the movies and there's the perfect seat available and no one else is in the theater except that one other person who respects the rule about turning off your phone and not talking during the movie."

I ask if he thought of that because we're on the roof of a movie theater. Kat and Irene each punch one of my arms. They're fucking strong. My arms are throbbing. I want to cry, but this is Clark's moment. I can't be selfish.

"Yeah. So?"

"It's ok, Clark," Kat says. "We're listening."

"I don't know, man. I just really wish I'd have said goodbye to her, told her how I really felt about her, told her I wish we hadn't've lost contact. Maybe I wouldn't have killed myself." He breaks out into another bout of sobbing. We just let him. I think he'll tire himself out or something and just, like, go to sleep but he's dead and doesn't sleep so he just keeps crying and we keep freezing until the girls have the bright idea to do something about it. They suggest we track down Sarah, find out where she lives and see if we can maybe somehow say goodbye to her from Clark. It seems like a good idea. Like I said, I like having Clark around and this seems like the decent thing to do. If I was a ghost and miserable and forced to stick with some dude I didn't know for all eternity, it'd be cool if he did something nice for me every once and a while.

I go, "Yeah, let's do it. Do you remember where she lived?"

"Chino," he says.

"Where's that?"

"California."

We borrow a car from some guy the girls knew. Well, technically, we steal it, but we promise we'll bring it back after he calls the girls up threatening to go to the cops or call their stepdad. We tell him that it's for a good cause and that by not calling the cops or their stepdad he's helping someone pass over to the other side. He says we're all fucking nuts but we have one week and if his car isn't back in one week then it'll be off to the slammer for me and off to whatever their stepdad has planned for them. Sounds good. Sounds fair. Thanks, guy!

It only takes us a few days to get to Chino. We take turns driving, all of us but Clark even though he volunteers. I say we should let him, but the girls say they didn't want to risk dying and being stuck with me too. That's fair. Throughout the whole trip, Clark talks about Sarah. About how pretty she is. Her eyes are a shade of blue he'd never seen before or that he thinks has even been discovered. Her lips do this cute little twitch when she gets scared or nervous. Her hair is like a sunset. He talks about how kind she is to everyone she met, how she had donated her kidney to some random person she'd never even met because that's just who she is. He talks about all the things they did growing up: bonfires at the beach, Disneyland trips, baseball games, pool parties, etc. etc.

"Is she a psychic like us?"

Clark thinks about it. "I don't think so."

"Bummer. Thought maybe she'd be able to see you if she was. Maybe we'll get lucky and she's a witch or something. They see ghosts, too. Was she a witch?"

"Probably not," he says.

When we get to Chino, we go to the last place he remembers her living. It's a small apartment complex. There's an empty pool in the middle of the complex and four palm trees at the corners of the pool. The place looks kind of sketchy, but we'll do anything for love. We knock on the door. No one answers. We knock again. No dice. We knock on a neighbor's door and an old man comes out wearing a Hawaiian shirt and white underwear. He looks like the guy I used to buy my weed from before my brain went ka-blooey and I forgot who he was and where to find him so I could buy more weed. LOL!

Kat tosses her hair back, "Hi, sir. I love your shirt. Is the person who lives at this apartment named Sarah?"

The old man looks us up and down and up and down. "No. Only person who lives there is Chuck. Fuck Chuck," he says, goes back inside.

"Chuck sounds like a fucking douche," I say.

We leave the apartment complex with the empty swimming pool and palm trees and try a few more places where Clark says he thinks maybe possibly Sarah lives at or has lived. There's a small house with two big dogs that aren't as cute as the DMV puppies. That house belongs to a young family with four babies and marital problems. There's a bigger house that's abandoned and looks like it's been seized by the cops or something because there's orange tape everywhere and it smells like chemicals. There's another apartment complex that's much newer and has new paint and new stucco and a new gate and new security cameras and a new tennis court and a new gym and new tenants because Sarah doesn't live there anymore and we're trespassing so get the fuck out of here, the security guard tells us, but he's super fat and we laugh and while the girls distract him, I steal his flashlight and we book it. The girls and I think it's the funniest thing we've ever seen and/or done, but Clark gets super bummed. Nothing is working out and nothing is pointing us in the right direction to where Sarah might be. Clark wants to kill himself all over again. Oof. Super bummer.

"Clark, is there anywhere else you think she might be," I ask.

We drive around for a long time going absolutely nowhere. That's pretty much what being alive is, right? Just moving moving moving, not knowing where the fuck you're going until you don't have anywhere else to go. Then, it's all over and you move on or your stay behind like Clark. Fuck, everything is so sad.

"I really thought we'd find her by now," Clark says.

It starts raining and the cars on the freeway stop moving because that's what happens when it rains in California, I guess. Dark clouds blanket themselves on the mountains north of the 60 West. The darker it gets, the more alive Clark looks.

"If I could hug you right now, I would," Irene tells Clark. "You deserve a hug."

Clark gives a pathetic smile.

We get off the freeway, take the side streets of whatever city we're in. People are huddled together beneath the overpasses, waiting out the rain and the thunder and the lightning. Taco stands hustle down the sidewalk to get out from under the rain and the thunder and the lightning. Everyone afraid of being alone. Everyone afraid of something.

The hostess at the diner tells us to sit wherever. Okay. Diners are always better when it's raining, you know? Hot coffee and pie and rain. You've got to enjoy the simple things before they're gone. The waitress comes over to take our orders.

"Sarah," Clark says, voice cracking.

I mean, I don't want to shit on Clark's memories or anything, but she isn't everything he described her to be. Maybe that's what love is, though. Maybe love is seeing what isn't there or what is there that no one else is able to see. Maybe that's all that matters.

Kat asks, "Did you know a guy named Clark?"

Sarah says, "Clark *who?*"

"Stevens," Clark says.

"Clark Stevens," I say. "Can I get a coffee with Baileys if you have any?" Irene gives me a dirty look, punches my arm.

Clark looks like a kid about to lose his virginity on prom night, excited and nervous and about to puke. He fixes the collar on his polo shirt like he expects Sarah to wake from some trance and see him.

"Hold on. Clark Stevens?" She lets out a gross laugh. "You mean, Greasy Clark?"

Clark deflated. Clark defeated. Clark dead all over again.

"I haven't thought about that guy in forever! He was such a weirdo. How do you know him?"

The room goes arctic with Clark.

"He said you were friends," Kat says.

Sarah puts her notepad in her apron pocket. "Clark was sweet when we were little kids but then when we got older, in high school or whatever, he got creepy. He started growing out that ponytail. Ew. That's when everyone started calling him 'Greasy Clark'. We all thought he was a stalker or a pedophile or something."

"Why?"

"I don't know. Like I said, he was just weird. What the hell is he up to these days? Does he still have that ponytail? Please tell me he got rid of it."

I blurt it out, scream it. "Clark's dead." The whole diner shuts the fuck up and turns to our table. Clark looks shellshocked.

Sarah opens her mouth probably to say something fucking stupid.

"Yeah," Kat says. "Clark's dead. He died a hero. There was this fire, and Clark and a bunch of other people were stuck inside the building where the fire was."

Irene jumps in, "There was a bunch of kindergarteners. And the building was an animal shelter. Clark kicked open the fucking door like goddamn Captain America and carried every single kid and every single puppy and every single animal to safety."

Oohs and ahhs fill the background. Everyone listens. Everyone cares. Everyone honoring Clark. Everyone respecting Clark.

"The building collapsed on Clark as he went in to make sure it was cleared out. He didn't survive. He died. He died a motherfucking hero," Irene says.

"We're his best friends. Clark is our idol. We worship Clark. And his ponytail was the raddest fucking ponytail that ever existed," Kat screams.

Clark shines bright like a million stars bursting into existence.

I can't think of anything cool to add to the story of Clark's heroic death. So, I just yell, "One time I kissed Clark by accident and now I'll never love anyone again." It feels right. I regret nothing.

We leave the diner right as Sarah burst into tears. I hope she's still crying and will continue to cry until the end of time. When we're all ashes and dust and the universe is jelly. Fuck it. I hope she's still crying even after that.

The road back home is quiet. The good kind of quiet, you know? The serene kind of quiet. The quiet that happens when it's done raining and the sun peaks out from behind charcoal clouds and goes, oh hey it's me, I'm back! Clark sits next to me in the backseat, staring out the window, a big stupid smile across his face. Blissful and wanting for nothing. Kat asks if we can pull over and sleep for a while. Just a little while. Just half an hour. Just until we feel a little more rested.

"You guys deserve to rest," Clark says.

We pull over next to the desert. The sun sinks behind a sea of cacti and emptiness. We sleep for however long we sleep for. It's a while, though. The sun hangs blazing and vivid in the sky above us. The car is warm. Like sheets out of the dryer. Like a bonfire at the beach. Like whiskey in the morning. Like going home.

Clark is gone.

That Wolf Motherfucker

It pretty much started with him howling during orgasm on top of his girlfriend one night. After that, he grew a mustache. He'd never had a mustache. Thick red follicles spread from his eyebrows to his forehead, down his neck and shoulders and back and all the places. He switched from a plant-based diet and went full carnivore. Steak and eggs and pork. His depression went away. Libido through the roof. His girlfriend noticed.

"You're more bite than bark," she'd joke.

He'd roll his eyes. Cliché. Whatever.

The neighbor's dog stopped shitting in his lawn, it wouldn't even come outside anymore.

Now, he'd shit in their lawn. Big heaping, smelly dumps. He'd shit bones.

He started fighting MMA. Called Joe Rogan a little bald bitch. He won all the belts, even the ones outside of his weight division. They let him fight whoever and whenever he wanted.

Sponsors poured in. Money, too. He paid off his mom's house and medical bills.

"Come visit me," his mom said.

He did. But the rest of his family couldn't stand to be around him. They said he'd changed; they said he was different, he was all wrong.

His girlfriend moved out. Couldn't stand the smell.

Snow fell like static, covered everywhere. Ice clung to everything. A scorching white blanket stretched on and on and on. A man would go blind. He heard their calls ahead, stripped naked and ran like a motherfucker.

Blood tonight, he thought. His eyes black as nightmares.

Rat-Gator-Human

It started when the pinks called the purples a bunch of egocentric twats and the purples got pissed and they both started falling and swirling into madness and eating each other and crying and oof, it was just bad, man. That's basically when the sky went to shit. It bled shimmering gold blood onto the streets, and no one knew what the fuck to do except take cover and hope the sky would resolve its issues before whoopsie daisy, we're all dead. Thousands of people fled into subways and sewers and cellars, going deep deep deep underground, far away from the fighting and far away from the pink and purple sky and the sun and the stars and light in general. For a long time everyone walked around in the pitch-black underworld, getting concussions from running into walls or off ledges until their finally eyes adjusted. The new world was grey and wet and dirt-smeared and smelled like turds.

Someone would ask, "When do you think we can go back?"

Someone else would say, "What's there to go back to?"

The people made treaties with the rat kingdoms and the alligator nations and promised not to kill them or eat them or anything the way they killed and ate the animals above before the sky went to shit and there was nowhere left to go. The only food people could eat was whatever grew between the cracks in the cement and sometimes a four-eyed fish or something that swam into the tunnels and pipes that the alligators and rats looked at and were like, nah, bro, that's all you.

A hundred years or a thousand years (kinda hard to keep track of time without the sky, you know?) passed and somewhere along the way someone fucked an alligator and got pregnant and gave birth to a half-human/half-alligator and someone else fucked a rat and got pregnant and gave birth to a half-human/half-rat and then those two people fucked and Jesus Christ, man. But, anyway, yeah, there was a whole new species and they were fucking wild! They didn't give a shit about anyone's peace treaties or any of that because their brains were wired different, man. You remember that movie *The Hills Have Eyes* and how fucked up those people were? Pfft, it's not even close.

The Rat-Gator-Human species ate what was left of the human population. They started with the strongest of the humans, taunting them, goading them into fist/paw/limb fights. They'd let the humans win at first and then they'd chomp chomp chomp on their necks, blood going all gushy gushy. Sick. After they picked off the warriors or what-ever, they pretty much just ate whoever was left, wherever they found them, whenever they wanted. It was kinda sad but oh well, evolution, right? So long, mankind!

The rat kingdom and alligator nations made an alliance to try and put a stop to the Rat-Gator-Humans. They didn't want to have an all-out war, so they went stealth-mode and attacked the Rat-Gator-Humans. It looked like they were going to win for a minute because they knew the underworld way better and they had more experience with fighting and all that. They took out two pods (everyone called them 'pods') in a matter of a couple of days. Like, a couple hundred Rat-Gator-Humans. Supposedly, those pods held a lot of what you'd call their leaders, even though they didn't really have leaders. Rat-Gator-Humans were pretty fucking chaotic. Pretty punk rock. Pretty metal. Badass. Yeah! But the Rat-Gator-Humans caught on and went after the alligator nations and the rat kingdom and there was just no stopping them. No way. No how. Sorry. Not sorry. Adios, losers.

With the rats and the gators and the humans all gone, the Rat-Ga-tor-Humans had nothing left to eat and they wouldn't eat each other because despite being anarchists and lunatics, they had a code, man. I mean, fuck. Come on! The years (millennia?) went by and there was less and less to do and less and less to eat and the Rat-Gator-Humans kept on fucking and kept on reproducing and the underworld got so populated that they had to move deeper and deeper underground, boring into the earth until they were just a few miles from its core. They figured out a way to farm fish from the ocean without getting flooded. They figured out how to build condos and apartment complexes and neighborhoods and schools and factories. They had space. They had food. They had heat. They had jobs and education and opportunity. They all pitched in and helped each other out. They gave up on anarchy and were more or less into socialism. Everyone was super chill.

You probably already know how the next part goes because it's how it always goes and who knows if it'll ever go any other way: war, greed, gods, little bitty itty bitty baby dicks mad about their little bitty itty bitty baby dicks, disease, money, poverty, borders, etc. Yeah, super sad.

And that's when it started: the iron and the nickel started fighting with the platinum and uranium. The magma couldn't handle that kind of emotional stress and seemed like it was going to blow. The Rat-Gator-Humans fought and clawed and stepped on each other's necks to get back to the surface of the planet in hopes that the elements would work everything out before Earth went KA-BOOM!

The entire Rat-Gator-Human population crawled on the ground, shielding their eyes from the orange sun, having never seen light.

Someone would ask, "When can we go back?"

Someone else would say, "What's there to go back to?"

When they could see again, the Rat-Gator-Humans were met by Cobra-Grizzly-Humans that were a product of the humans who weathered the great shitstorm in the sky while the other humans fled underground.

They made treaties with the Cobra-Grizzly-Humans and promised not to kill them or eat them or anything the way they had killed and eaten the rats and the alligators and the humans below before the core went to shit and there was nowhere left to go.

Look-See

Aw, shit. Now, watch this. Look, see that big dude walking up? The one with the neck tattoo of the mermaid spreading her tail to look like she's a normal lady spreading her legs? Yep, yep. That's Buck Ritchie. Now, maybe you might never have heard of Buck Ritchie or maybe you might have heard a few things about Buck Ritchie but I'm gonna tell you something else you definitely haven't heard about him. No one has. No one except me, you understand? And once I tell you this, it's not to be repeated to any living soul on this plane of existence, you understand? This is solely for your benefit—shit, your protection—and nothing more. I don't want to hear this coming from nobody else's flappy fucking lips after I tell you what you need to know—what nobody wants you to know—about Buck Ritchie.

I had to learn this the hard way. There's hard, and then there's *hard*, and motherfucker the lesson I learned was goddamn *hard*. Three and a half years I hid Steve Crouch's shed when I learned what I know. Three and a half years I ate bugs and mice and drank my own piss. I came back to the world a new man. Everyone who's anyone will tell you: I changed. I was born again. Like a soldier come back from war. A new creature emerging from its chrysalis. A sinner made saint. The prodigal son.

See him go by? Yep, yep. Now, look at him really good. Take a good look. See how he's walking like that? Notice the left leg. Anything seem off to you about that left leg? Now, look at the right one. Uh-huh. You see it? You see it, right? Shit, that sonofabitch ain't like you and me. Thing is, he don't know I know. Oh, but brother, I know. You bet your sweet little asses I know. Learned it the hard way. I walked with the dead and communed with Death. I wrestled angels and butt-fucked demons. The lord Jesus Christ came down from the right hand of the father and snuffed out the last bit of innocence behind my eyes. My soul gone through the meat grinder. My hope hung on the noose.

Now, watch. See how he keeps his right hand in his pocket. Look! Did you catch that? The smallest movements give away so much. Shit, it's right in front of everyone. They can't accept it, though. Never could. Blind! All of them. Blind! Not me, though. I see now. And you'll see it, too. You're gonna thank me. You'll be grateful. More gratitude than you can imagine. Swear to God. You'll see Buck Ritchie for who—what!— he really is. And you'll know. You'll know what I know. What I've been knowing. I've known it for so long. Kept his secret all to myself, though he don't know it. A man isn't made to hold these kinds of secrets to himself. Fuck that shit. It'll make a man crazy. I been drove crazy. My mind shattered into a million pieces. Superglued together with a child's tears. Strung together with rusted wire. I saw all of me break apart, strewn across the universe. All of creation duplicated a billion times a billion times over and again. Big bang. Big crunch. KA-BOOM! That was my mind. I been enlightened. I been humbled. My ego been dead. Died and resurrected, hallelujah! You will too. You will too. You will too. You will too. You will too. You will too. You will too. You will too. You will too. You will too. You will too. You will too. You will too. You will too. You will too. You will too.

Now, watch this. Look, see that big dude walking up? The one with the neck tattoo of the mermaid spreading her tail to look like she's a normal lady spreading her legs? Yep, yep. That's Buck Ritchie.

Snow Globes & Black Holes

Every morning when I go downstairs to check the mail, I see my neighbor. I get no mail, just a whoosh of air that burst forth from my little box numbered 223. They removed my name from the box and just left the number. They didn't tell me, they just did it. I am nameless, faceless. A number only. No one will remember me. Ah, well. Every morning after I go downstairs to check the mail, my neighbor and I go back to my apartment and spend the rest of the day getting high. His name is Bill or Chris or Ripper or something. Who knows? Neither of us has a job or a retirement plan or health insurance. I dropped out of college a long time ago. Sometimes I steal things. Sometimes I imagine what dying feels like. Maybe I'll never know. We get high and watch the world that may or may not exist from my window. The people below us carry their imaginary groceries to their imaginary homes. They hold imaginary hands of people they're in imaginary love with. They give birth to imaginary babies who'll live imaginary lives and do extraordinary imaginary things. Or maybe they'll move into my apartment complex. Maybe they'll meet me and my neighbor Chris (?) and get high every day and we can all stare out my window together the way the universe wanted it to be.

My neighbor who I see every day goes missing. No one knows where he's gone. I ask around. People shrug and go, who? You know, Bill (?), I say. They shake their heads and pretend not to hear me. I don't know which apartment is his. His mailbox also only has a number: 213. We are all nameless. We are all imaginary.

I get high alone in my apartment and wonder if I'll die alone instead of with imaginary neighbors that may or may not be dead because people who go missing out of nowhere usually don't come back alive.

My father calls, asks when are you finishing your degree? When will you become a man? Did you know that you're a disappointment? Did you know I think I might hate you? My mother calls, says not to listen to my father. Says she's been praying for me. Every day. Every night. Asking God to help me out or something. Help me find my way. She thinks I'm lost but it's only a matter of time before I'm found, hallelujah! Debt collectors call and say, all your debt is going on your very real, totally not at all made-up credit report. Good luck trying to live a normal life, sucker! Many more people call, ask about my extended car warranty. It's nice that so many people care.

Two months pass. Maybe four. I don't know. I go to check my mail. A new neighbor in a suit and tie with a briefcase and a handsome smile has taken my missing neighbor's mailbox. I say hello, ask if he'd like to get high and watch the world that may or may not exist from my window. He pushes me against the other mailboxes, calls me a fucking loser, says don't bother him again or he'll cut my nuts off. Ouch.

I get high and watch the world that may or may not exist out my window. In front of the grocery store across the street, I see my neighbor, Ripper (?), waving his arms at me like one of those people who stand in the middle of landing strips and land airplanes. I see him, wave back.

I follow him behind the grocery store. He hugs me, squeezes tight. He has a beard now. Shrubbery of perfectly straight salt and pepper hair, waterfalling from chin to chest.

Cool beard, I say.

He goes, it itches.

Oh yeah? That can happen. I know this not because I have a beard but because I've been told this by people who do have beards. I don't have a beard. I've always wanted a beard. It's the only thing I've ever wanted, but I can't grow any facial hair. I tried once in my early twenties and my face looked like it was covered in blackheads. The coolest people have beards: Jerry Garcia, Plato, Jesus, Mick Foley—Mankind, Cactus Jack, Dude Love, et al.

He goes, you wanna see something horrible and wonderful?

I say, yes, I've always wanted to see something like that.

His eyes are dark. Darker than I remember. I don't really remember. I don't think I ever noticed. But they're fucking dark. Almost black. Black holes. I wonder where they'd take me. Surprise! You're on the other side of the galaxy now. Enjoy your stay! Windows to the soul, the eyes. Black holes, black souls. Ah, well. He stared at me, black eyes welling with tears, like he was surprised. Like he didn't think I'd say yes. Like he's asked a lot of people the same question that he just asked me and, for whatever reason, no one ever says yes. People are too scared. Or, maybe, people are just undecided. I'm both, truthfully, but his black hole eyes sucked me in. Whoosh! Here we go!

He walks me to a van that I assume is his parked behind the grocery store. An old Chevy Astro. A mixture of mustard yellow and diarrhea rust. Missing all but one hubcap. Duct-taped rear window. He says he lives here now. Nice. He keeps checking over his shoulder. I check over my shoulder. All clear. All good. He fumbles with the keys, slides open the door.

He goes, get in, hurry up. Closes the door behind him.

All the windows are blacked out. Like his eyes. Windows to the soul, windows to the Astro. He rustles through the unseeable things around us. The van sways back and forth the more he moves around, looking for whatever he's looking for. It's nice sitting in complete darkness with a mostly total stranger. But that's sort of what we do every day, right? Whether we're sitting at a window with a neighbor whose name we can't remember getting high or on a train or at church or in jail or a mental institution. I like being in this pitch-black van with my neighbor whose name I don't know. I feel in control knowing I'm not in control. Anything can happen. Maybe I'll wake up and I'll be a cartoon. Maybe I'll meet an alien. Maybe he'll kill me.

He flicks a BIC lighter and wow, look, thus the creation of the universe! He's sitting crisscross applesauce in front of me. I'm sitting that way, too. I didn't realize. Ah, well. The flame dances around in his black hole eyes. Stays dancing. Sways its hips and legs and look at it go! His other hand is holding something behind his back. I'm still fixated on the light in his eyes. Maybe this is a trick. Maybe he's holding the murder weapon behind his back. Dying like this wouldn't be so bad. There are worse ways to go. With me distracted, it would be easy to take me out with probably one or two blows. I'm not strong, either. I wouldn't be able to hold my own in a fight. I'm no Mick Foley.

He goes, I know how the world is going to end. He brings his other hand from around his back, sticks it out and shows me. An old, cracked snow globe that's been drained of the liquid and the snow and whatever little scene used to exist inside of it before it met its own end. He goes, look at it. I can't look at it anymore by myself. I can't be the only one who knows. Look hard and it'll show you. It'll show you how it happens. Tears cling to his eyes, the fire raging inside them.

I look hard and, sure enough, the end of everything swirled around in a cracked snow globe—he and I are sitting in a dark van, staring into a cracked snow globe, watching he and I sitting in a dark van, staring into a cracked snow globe, watching he and I sitting in a dark van, staring into a cracked snow globe, watching he and I sitting in a dark van, staring into a cracked snow globe, watching he and I sitting in a dark van, staring into a cracked snow globe, watching he and I, sitting in a dark van, staring into a cracked snow globe, watching he and I, sitting in a van, staring into a cracked snow globe, watching he and I, sitting in a dark van, staring into a cracked snow globe. Eternity passes through me.

He goes, you see?

Yeah, I see.

We hug and cry and I forget to ask him to remind me of his name.

I stand on my window ledge, waving at everyone below. Blowing kisses. Giving out thumbs up to everyone. My beard isn't just any old beard. I'm the wolf boy, covered in hair and fleas and howling at the moon. My neighbor, Archie (?), is opening portals to parallel universes, sending them letters of well wishes and congratulations for outlasting ours. There's a piano playing itself. It plays Happy Birthday to no one.

My phone rings. I throw it out the window, watch it break into a billion pieces. The people below fight over it. Above me, the sky is a mirror. It smiles down on me, says how proud it is of me. Says I've made it. I've reached Nirvana. Look at me go! I watch the flame dance around in my black hole eyes.

Piss Dreams

So, I have this dream where I'm at my grandma's house—I haven't been to my grandma's house in over ten years and, besides, she's dead—and I have to piss bad. Instead of going to the bathroom, though, I decide to start pissing behind one of the dressers in the guest bedroom. My grandma goes, "Fucking gross, dude! Don't piss on my carpet!" So, I go to the bathroom and piss there. Problem is, halfway through my piss, the color changes. I'm not pissing my usual neon yellow. I'm pissing straight crimson. Red piss. Blood. I start pissing blood. It's dark and thick and holy shit, man! It's bad.

I wake up having to piss in real life. I sit down on the toilet because images of blood dripping from my dick are running through my mind and I get super queasy when I think about blood so if I pass out I'd rather be sitting than standing. If I'm standing, I'll probably fall over and crack my head on the sink or some shit. Yikes! Anyway, yeah, I'm not pissing blood. I'm pissing regular piss, so it seems everything is totally fine and I'm just freaking out over a dream. So, go back to sleep. Relax, man. Everything is okay.

THE FUCK IT IS!

As soon as sunlight breaks through my kitchen windows, I'm on the phone trying to get in touch with my on-call psychic, Chuck. After thirty minutes of going straight to voicemail, Chuck finally picks up.

"What the fuck, Chuck?"

"I was talking to Jesus," she says.

Whatever. I tell her about my dream. About the blood and the piss and my grandma's house. I ask her what it all means.

Chuck says I have secrets. That I'm keeping things from the people in my life and that it's causing me great stress and tearing my soul apart. She says if I don't become a more honest person then it'll cost me everything I have, and I don't have much.

"I do have a lot of secrets," I say.

Chuck goes, "Yeah, yeah. Sort that shit out."

I call my old boss and ask if he'll meet me for a few drinks at a bar near the store he used to own that got turned into one of those CrossFit gyms. He says sure, but I'm buying because he fired me and I owe him that much. Ugh. Fine, man. Whatever. Yeah, sure. Okay. We meet at the bar. I'm twenty minutes late and he's already drunk.

"Listen, Rich. I'm really sorry to have to be the one to tell you this, but I'm trying to make sure I don't piss blood or anything." I wait to see if he'll show any sympathy for my hypothetical illness. None, yet. "I stole from your store."

He goes, "Yeah, numb-nuts. That's why I fired you."

"I mean, kinda. You fired me for the money you found out I stole. I kinda stole a lot more."

His big, blue bloodshot eyes well up with tears and fall down his fat, rosacea red cheeks like anvils in all of those old Wile E. Coyote cartoons.

The waiter comes over, asks what I'll be having. I tell him two beers, two shots, and a joint if he has one. He laughs. I don't.

Rich takes a fork, reaches across the table, drives it straight through my left hand. Yeah, okay. I deserved that. It's a solid drive, too. Like, I feel it in the nerves and around the bones and oh my fucking god that shit hurts! Rich looks happy or, at least, happier. Good for him.

Blood is pouring from my hand onto the table. I wrap one of the restaurant napkins around my hand, drop a few twenties. Goodbye, Rich!

"I'm gonna kill you," he says.

"Sounds like a plan," I say.

I call my ex-girlfriend, tell her that the rumors of me cheating on her were totally true, but not with the person everyone said I cheated on her with. I tell her that I boned her dad. He's a George Clooney-type and was in the middle of that nasty divorce with her mom and I felt really bad for him and it was weird because neither of us had ever felt that way before so, I mean, come on! It's whatever-year-it-is! She breaks a bottle of California red over my head. The blood drips ooey-gooey down my neck.

She goes, "Burn in hell!"

I go, "Will do!"

I'm bleeding from my hand, bleeding from my head. But, hey, at least I'm not bleeding from my dick, right!? I text my old drug dealer. Tell him I ratted him out to the cops. I'm the reason the cops raided his house and killed his cat. His favorite cat. He and a couple guys in a black SUV drive by, shoot up my house. I have a few through and throughs. Nothing major. Maybe a kidney or lung or something. It's cool, though. It was my bad. My fault. Whoops. So sorry.

No more secrets!

I call my doctor. "I never take my meds! Ha ha ha!" I say.

I call my credit card company. "I'm just gonna wait until the debt falls off my credit report in seven years. I ain't paying back shit!"

I call the IRS. "I don't have kids and I lie about how much I make on my taxes."

I call my best friend. "I don't think you should work it out with your wife. She hates you. You hate her. I know a good attorney."

I call the FDA. "I know what you're doing to all that 'organic' food!"

I call my neighbor who lives across from me. "Your husband is a Russian spy."

I call everyone I've ever known and some I've never met, spill the beans to everyone. My dentist. My third-grade teacher. The girl at the sandwich shop. My pharmacist. That lawyer I always see on television. The employees at the record store. The USPS. The Girl Scouts of America. The trashman. The guy who drove the ice cream truck through my neighborhood as a kid. He's dead. I leave a voicemail anyway. I call all the major news outlets. CNN. Fox News. PBS. Associated Press. Hold a press conference and tell them all my dirty little secrets. I write a personal Memoir—*Piss Dreams*—publish it on the world wide web.

Everyone everywhere knows everything about me. I have nothing to hide. No skeletons in my closet. No confidential information. No privacy. I've been chased through the streets. Shot at. Stabbed. Kidnapped for ransom ("G'head and kill him," they said). Poisoned. Infected with incurable diseases. Decapitated. Hung. Stretched. Disemboweled. Drawn and quartered. I'm a lot like Vigo the Carpathian from Ghostbusters II except I don't want to eat a baby or whatever it was he was trying to do.

Chuck doesn't answer when I call. She hates me, too. I leave a voicemail. "I did it," I say. "I have no more secrets."

I watch from the storm drain where I live now as strangers pass by, shrouded in mystery. They breathe in the air, soak in the sunlight. They smile and wave at one another politely. Hugs and kisses. Family dinners and proposals and graduation parties. Hiding in plain sight. Not me, though. No, not me. My blood turns black and my organs slowly decay and my heartbeat slows to a dull ka-thunk, ka-thunk, ka-thunk. I die in the darkness. Completely and totally free.

Trash People

The sheriff shows up with the landlord who has the eviction paperwork from the court that the judge has signed. It says we can't live here anymore. It's all really sad. They take our shit and throw it out the window and onto the street. Some kids set everything on fire, dance around it like in Lord of the Flies or something. Our whole lives a sacrifice to the apathetic gods above. Our couch. Our clothes. Our wedding vows. Our books. Our leftover pizza. Everything. Even part of our souls are down there, engulfed in flames.

Lucy says to the sheriff, fuck you, pig!

The sheriff punches Lucy in the mouth, punches me in the mouth, punches the landlord in the mouth, asks for the keys to the apartment. I put them between my knuckles like this, take a couple of jabs at his throat, watch the blood go down his neck in big globs. LOL! We run to my truck, peel out of the complex. So long, motherfuckers!

Lucy says we're free now. I think that's what she says. Honestly, I can't really understand her because her mouth is all swollen and my ears are ringing.

I tell Lucy that we're trash people now and we should move to the dump. She agrees. The rent is cheap and there's lots of room, too. Our new neighbors are great. They meet us at the front of the dump with all these weapons made from trash. A sword made out of an old computer keyboard. Nun chucks made out of stale bread and neckties. They tell us about a war brewing between the trash people and the non-trash people. Fuck yeah. We're in.

Lucy and I build our new home from an empty piano and an electric fireplace that still sort of works but might also explode and kill us. Shrug. Our new place has a view of the old place where we used to live. We can still see the smoke from all our stuff burning, reaching toward the sky, desperately escaping this life and crawling on to the next. The neon sign from the bar next door shines like the north star, like a miracle. Above us, nothing but haze and crows circling. It's like someone is smiling down on us. Amen.

Gareth is our closest neighbor. He lives in the porta-potty across from us. A chemical fire years ago burned off all of his body hair, so now he's convinced he's a snake. Slithering on the ground, going sssssssss sssssssss sssssssss. Like that. Maybe that has nothing to do with the fire, though. IDK. Maybe he's always believed he's a snake. I think people can be whoever they want to be. Free country and all.

Lucy says, good for you, man—snakes are rad as shit.

We let him bite us once. He's been cool ever since. Everyone just kind of keeps to themselves, does their own thing. Live and let live kind of shit. There's no malls or coffee shops or theme parks in the dump. No tourists, either. If you're in the dump, it's because you're a trash person and you deserve to live here like everyone else who deserves to live here. It's real peaceful.

One night we hear some ka-whomp ka-whomp of something big flying overhead. We peak our heads out. It's the United States Army descending down on us, guns a-blazing. They shoot and kill everyone they see. Gareth hisses at us to follow him. We do. We slither underneath towers of trash, deep underground through a narrow dirt tunnel. After what feels like hours, the ceiling is high enough that we can stand. Ahead of us, the tunnel forks.

I tell Gareth, lead the way.

He says, sssssssssssorry. You're not a sssssssssnake. You go the other way.

I asked where that leads to.

He shrugs.

Okay. Thanks, Gareth.

Lucy and I take the other tunnel, walk real slow in the pitch black, feeling the walls, hoping we don't fall off a cliff and die. An orange light grows in the distance. We see more of the tunnel, start walking faster, faster, faster. We run toward the orange light. We hear voices, laughter and singing. The ground starts to incline higher and higher. Our legs feel like they're going to explode. We need to work out more often. The orange light gets brighter. The tunnel gets hotter. So hot we start sweating. I mean, we're dripping buckets. We get to the edge of the tunnel, look up at the light. We're standing directly underneath a large wooden effigy. The flames scream in agony and madness. Lucy starts crying, points ahead.

Everything we left behind, everything we lost is there within the raging fire.

I want to go home, she says.

We hold hands, step out of the tunnel and back into the fire. The flames envelop us as we take back what's ours.

Juice

We buy goldfish. Just one. From the pet store at the mall. It's Wednesday. The fish tank won't get here until next week, so I use a casserole dish that somebody left at the funeral reception. The goldfish swims back and forth like it's running up and down a football field.

"His name is Juice," my son says.

"Why Juice?"

"Because if I drink it, I think it'll taste like orange juice."

Smartest fucking kid alive.

He feeds the goldfish this flakey cardboard shit that says it's specifically designed for optimum goldfish health. Swim faster. Hold its breath longer. Etc. The goldfish pops its head up to the top of the casserole dish, sucks the cardboard flakes down. Belly full, it just kinda floats there lethargic and high. A long black turd pokes out from its tail, wades in the water. Shit follows you wherever you go. It's only natural. Fish, human, whatever. No escaping it.

We moved out here, out in the middle of fucking nowhere, because of some of the shit that follows me. Like, how my son's mom OD'd while he was asleep one night. I found her on the toilet the next morning. That follows me. Follows my son, too.

Every morning, my son hops out of his sleeping bag, checks on the goldfish. "Juice isn't dead," he says. "Can I feed it?"

"Yeah, buddy. Go for it. Just a pinch, though. Don't want it getting too fat."

He eyeballs the cardboard flakes between his fingers, measuring whatever he thinks might be too much or too little, sprinkles it over the goldfish. Good job, buddy. Whenever Juice pops its little fish lips out of the water to snag a flake, my son smiles all proud. He is the giver and keeper of life.

I wake up one morning and see he's not in his sleeping bag. His sleeping bag isn't in his room. I call his name. No call back. Bathroom empty. Living room empty. I check the kitchen. He's lying in his sleeping bag, curled up next to the fridge. I nudge him.

"Hey, buddy. Why are you sleeping out here?"

He keeps his eyes closed. "Juice is dead. I'm gonna bring it back to life."

I look on the counter for the fish. No sign of the casserole dish. No goldfish, either.

"What? Where's Juice?"

"Right now, Juice is dead. But I read about people being cryogenically frozen so they can come back to life one day. So, that's what I'm doing with Juice." He points to the fridge.

I open the freezer. The casserole dish sits on top of the frozen corn dogs. Juice stares out, eyes warbled and wide, a perfectly preserved orange epidermis under a shiny slime coat. I think of Walt Disney. I imagine his frozen head on Juice's body. Ha!

My son reaches in, grabs the makeshift fishbowl and sets it on the kitchen counter. A smile inches from ear to ear. He is the giver and taker of life.

I break the news to him. "I think we'll have to throw Juice in the trash."

He looks up like, the fuck? "No. I told you, I'm bringing Juice back to life," he tells me, staring me down like, try and do something, motherfucker. I dare you.

It's freezing inside and it's freezing outside. We sit all day watching the ice melt slowly. Or maybe it's not melting. Hard to tell. We watch our frozen goldish melting or not melting at all. Either way, we're spending quality time together. That's cool. I'd murder all the goldish in the entire world to sit next to him like this. To feel my love for him explode and create new galaxies every time he looks up and says, "Just wait, dad. Stay with me and watch. You'll see." And I don't want to do anything but sit with him forever. To be frozen like the goldfish, perfectly healthy and happy. The only good shit in my life lasting forever and ever until an asteroid destroys us. Even then, we'd still be together.

The sun has fallen behind the end of the earth and the moon is somewhere on the other side of the apartment building next to us. A breeze knocks steadily against the kitchen window. One of our neighbors is listening to Garbage. I fall asleep, chin buried in the enclave of my chest.

Little fists reign fire on my ribs. "Dad! Look!"

Pain shoots up and down and across my neck. I'm paralyzed. No, wait. I slept in a chair and I'm fucking old. Give me a minute.

"Look at Juice! Look at Juice!"

Son of a bitch. It's alive. Swimming with a stupid fucking fish grin across its fish face. Like it never realized it was frozen. Or it did and it's happy it's not anymore. Though, goldfish have short memories so I don't know. Whatever. Juice is alive. And it's swimming in my casserole dish like nothing ever happened. Many happy returns, Juice! Welcome back.

"Holy shit," I say.

My son says, "Yeah. Holy shit."

We watch Juice. A second chance at life. Fucking wow!

"Let's go, Dad." He pulls my arm hard. He's already got his pants and coat and boots and scarf on.

I rub my neck, try to work through the pain. "Don't you want to hang out with Juice?"

"No! Let's go!" His voice breaks, tears fill his eyes.

"Where are we going?"

"To get mom."

Birds Aren't Real

My girlfriend tells me something's off in our relationship. Says we're missing a spark or magic or whatever she calls it.

I go, oh, you wanna see magic?

She goes, yeah, idiot, I just said that.

So, I wrap an old t-shirt around her eyes and lead her out into the field behind our apartment. It's all a big surprise. The ice chest is full of beers and pastrami sandwiches and the chocolate cookies she baked last month. I put a slice of bread in a Ziplock bag with the cookies to keep them fresh. The cookies stay moist and soft, and the bread gets dry and ugly. Success!

We're walking for a while when she says her feet hurt. There's always something to complain about, isn't there? A little foot pain never killed anyone. Sometimes you've gotta pay the price. Magic ain't free, you know. The hum of electricity gets louder, ricocheting off the clouds the closer we get.

I tell her we're here and take the shirt off her eyes. See? There they are, I say, pointing.

Just look at those things — all perched up on the powerlines without a goddamn care in the world. Dozens of them in rows, twisting their necks and heads, fluttering their wings, cooing, cooing and cawing, cawing.

She goes, the fuck is this?

I go, It's *magic*!

Those are just birds.

I drop the ice chest, hear one of the cans spray open inside. *Just birds?* There's no way you're serious. If you're being serious, you're out of your mind.

She stares at me, then the birds, then me.

I put my hands on her shoulders, look at her real seriously, and drop the motherfucking truth-bomb: *Birds aren't real.*

A hawk circles above us. It swoops down, grabs a rat or snake or something, flies off with it into the blue picture screen above us.

Wait, she says. You mean, like, we're living in a simulation — the Matrix or something? I shake my head no, gulping one of the beers that busted open in the ice chest.

Not at all, I tell her. People who think shit like that are just weird. I mean the birds aren't real.

She reaches in the ice chest, grabs the Ziplock bag of cookies and walks back toward our apartment.

So much for magic, I yell.

I'm six or seven beers deep, watching the birds chill on the power-lines, watching the clouds pass, listening to the wind and the electricity intertwine and envelop me in my own little cocoon.

One of the birds asks, what's your problem, dude?

I sit up, swig my beer. I don't have a problem, I say.

Thirty or so of them all turn their heads to me like the ticking of the long hand on a clock.

The powerlines stop humming. They go, oh yeah? Then why'd you tell her we're not real? All their beaks move, one voice, stereo, super cool. What's your angle, friend? We're as real as you.

Horse shit! I'm flesh and blood. My heart beats like a steady drum. There's poison in my veins. When I sleep, I dream, I nightmare. You, you're a fraud. And you know it. You're an illusion of the mind. And you can't convince me otherwise.

The birds levitate from the wires, fly in a furious circle. Their feathers fling from their bodies, become liquid, like hot magma, forming an ooey gooey black blanket, snuffing out the sun. They cover me, a big bubble of darkness and energy. It sort of reminds me of that Pauly Shore movie, Bio-Dome, but better. A hologram of my girlfriend rises beneath me. She looks super pissed. Very realistic. Her hips start shaking and her eyes roll into the back of her head, shine bright neon pink. I'm into it. Dance with me, she says.

I throw my hands in the air, I don't even care. My legs move this way and that, shaking my shit like I know what to do with it.

She smiles wide, wide, wider. Birds with wings of fire fly out from behind her teeth, straight at me like bullets. I duck and cover. The echo of their screeching — radio static. I look up at my hologram girlfriend. She flaps her arms, flies away.

I stand there, not knowing who I like better: my hologram girlfriend or my real girlfriend. My feet feel warm. I look down, I'm standing on a powerline. It sizzles like a plate of fajitas. My tennis shoes are melting. The skin around my toes goes drip, drip, drip. I watch it fall into the abyss below.

A tornado of birds surrounds me, screaming: It's not real. You're not real. They're not real. It's so not, not! We're not real. What is real? Are you really surely real? Who, then? For reals?

One of the birds comes and sits on my shoulder. It's heavy. Like, weighs as much as I weigh kind of heavy. I can't hold my balance, slip and fall into the abyss. I land on a giant slice of white bread, sink inside. A giant hand reaches at me, grabs a giant cookie, retracts. I'm in the Ziplock bag. Light expands and I see my real girlfriend sitting at our white IKEA kitchen table, crying, with chocolate smeared at the corners of her mouth. I never noticed how messy of an eater she is. I shout her name. She doesn't hear me. My insides shrivel, dry out. My tongue turns to crust. I am dry, dead bread. Her hand reaches in, grabs me. Our kitchen walls scroll by like a movie in fast-forward, then I'm falling down, down, down. I reach the bottom of the trashcan. The lid closes and it's back to black.

I can't open my eyes because one of the birds crapped on my face. It smells like a nursing home or a bar right after closing. I wipe it away with the shirt my girlfriend left before she went back to the apartment. The ice chest is upside down, ice spilled over and melted. Empty beer cans everywhere, suds on the lips. Sandwiches gone. The powerlines hum quietly. Stars shine down on the wet grass. And those fucking birds? They're still there. I pick up my things, head home.

There's a note on the counter. It says, I can't do this anymore. I'm sorry. There's leftovers in the fridge. Take care of yourself. I crumple the note, throw it in the trash, next to the rotten piece of bread.

One Note

We've been on the side of the road for, like, three hours or something. We're supposed to be opening for this shitty goth band in someone's living room in the middle of nowhere. We're drinking all that's left of the beer and coming up with our story instead. No one's called to let the guy, Paul or whoever-the-fuck, know we're not gonna make it.

Tom takes a big swig of his beer, eyes glossy, and goes, "Yeah, so, Alex, your girlfriend fucked some dude that you used to be friends with and so you got really high on PCP and shit yourself and tried to jump out of the van."

Alex throws an empty can at Tom's face. "Fuck you, bro. I'm not saying I shit myself. That's fucking stupid."

I hold in a scream. Ami gives me a look like, don't. We're drunk. We're over this. We've been over this for a while. Our band sucks. This van sucks. Everything sucks. I love Ami and she loves me. We haven't told anyone, even each other. We're gonna quit the band and get married and have a dozen babies and live in a haunted prison and make a vegetable garden and plant a bunch of oak trees to keep the rest of the world out and pretend we're the only people alive on the whole planet and the whole planet is just our little home forever and ever. Ha!

We're on the side of the road because we ran out of gas and we're stranded. That's it. Tom was driving and thought we were closer to a gas station than we really were. So, this is Tom's fault. Tom's trying to blame it on Alex. I don't know where the PCP bit comes from. Tom is always coming up with shit. Like, one time Tom missed band practice because he said he was getting a hummer from three chicks who thought he was this other guy in this other band none of us had ever heard of. But actually he went to visit his grandma because she was about to die.

The cops show up, give us each a sobriety test. Ami and I fail but the cop is too lazy to arrest us. Says we're not worth the paperwork and blah blah. He calls roadside assistance, tells us get the fuck out of his county before we decide to wrap ourselves around a tree or something. He doesn't feel like cleaning up the mess. Mmmkay

AAA refills our tank and we're on our way. Tom drives, pissed. Alex is pissed at Tom who is driving. Ami is perfect. I'm ready for all of this to be over.

"We're going to that fucking party," Tom says.

"Good. You can tell them you shit yourself and that's why we're late," Alex says.

The party is still happening. There's punks and goths and kids in polos and kids who look like kids drinking shit that kids shouldn't drink but they end up drinking anyway just because they're kids and don't want to be. Tom starts kissing Paul whoever-the-fuck's ass and apologizing for us not being there. Paul says it's no big deal, we suck and everyone would've hated us anyway. That breaks Tom's heart. He plays it off like it's a real good joke. Like Paul's a real funny guy. Ha. Ha. Funny, right? Paul tells us to enjoy ourselves.

Some all-girl punk band is screaming about their cunts and pro-phetic dreams. The lead singer strips off all her clothes and covers her tits in peanut butter. A dude next to me says their set's just started. He tells me that the bassist sometimes eats out the lead singer mid-set. All the guys are standing around, waiting to see if it's true. Ami and I go outside to smoke cigarettes.

"You think the bassist will really eat out the lead singer," I ask.

"Who cares? It'd be cooler if she ate herself out."

"Yeah. That'd be fucking sick."

A fight breaks out between two goth kids and two kids in polo shirts. The kids in polo shirts kick the shit out of the goth kids. One of the goth kids starts crying, begging the kids in the polo shirts to stop, please, stop, please, please, please. Then the goth kid pulls a bottle out of his coat, smashes it against the face of one of the kids in the polo shirts who then hits the ground, screaming bloody murder, blood gushing between his fingers. The goth kids run off into the woods behind the house as the girlfriends or sisters or both of the kids in the polo shirts chase after them.

"This is the best night," I say.

"It's only gonna get better," Ami says.

We go back inside, grab a bottle of tequila from the kitchen, watch the rest of the all-girl punk band. No one eats anyone out. The dudes are super bummed.

Tom is trying to convince Paul whoever-the-fuck to let us play. Alex is trying to convince Tom to let it go. Drink the free booze, find a chick to hook up with, shut the fuck up. Tom says fine, whatever. Goes off and sulks in an armchair by himself. Ami smokes a joint with him. He gets high, feels better. I love her. I want to watch fire cascade on the planet. As everyone suffers, agony and misery ravaging everyone, I want to look into her eyes, feel her knife scrape my ribs and puncture my heart. Feel her rip my soul from my body. Tear it into a million pieces and fling it out off a mountaintop like cremated ashes. I want her to drink my blood, spit it out into the void of space.

Paul whoever-the-fuck gets on the microphone. "Excuse me, everyone."

No one pays attention. Everyone is too busy getting drunk or high or fucking or fighting or running in the middle of nowhere, shrouded in darkness.

"Everybody shut the fuck up and listen to me," he yells.

Fine.

"There's one final act tonight." He motions to this short little fucker standing behind him. The short dude stands behind his keyboard, just high enough that his nose is visible above the keys. He stands on his tippy toes, pulls the microphone down.

"This guy's so fucking good," Ami says.

"I can't wait," I say.

The guy goes, "Thank you for your sacrifice," and hits a single note. Something between a low-octave Bb and a low-octave Eb. And he just fucking stays there. The note drifts out from the speakers, circles like smoke on the ceiling, sits still. It hangs there unmoving. Every living thing in the room watches, slack jawed and stupid.

The short dude presses his mouth on the microphone and goes, "Wow." His voice warbled and abysmal.

Screams expand through the air that's left in the house. One by one, souls leave their bodies. Eyes pop from skulls like eggs on a skillet. The screams mutate, turn to laughter. Air in lungs turns to gasoline. Fire catapults from mouths. Bodies fall like drivel, melt into pools of goop. Babies with black eyes climb out of the puddles.

Ami holds my hand. She reaches up, kisses me. "This is all for us," she says.

That Was the Dream

John had this recurring dream where he was a skyscraper. Tallest in the world. All the other skyscrapers looked up to him. Literally and the other way. He protected the smaller skyscrapers by stepping on the meaner, douchier ones. Then, he'd pick up the douchescrapers and break them in half. Everyone loved him. Inside, everyone who couldn't afford a place of their own was given one of those fancy apartments you'd find in Manhattan or Los Angeles. John also had the world's leading hospital inside of him. No one ever died. They lived forever. All diseases were cured. God lived inside of John, too. But he mostly kept to himself. Everyone just thought it was cool that God lived in their building, you know? John was pretty stoked about it, too. Everything beautiful inside of John, everyone happy and fulfilled. And he held them up effortlessly. As long as he was around, everything was good. Life was good. Worth living. John had the power, man. All the power.

Every time John woke up from that dream, he wanted to kill himself. He wanted to kill himself because being a skyscraper was unrealistic and even in a metaphorical sense, there was no chance that John would ever be that happy. That was the real dream: happiness.

So John volunteered for one of those studies where they lock you away in a big grey building for an unspecified amount of time. They paid two hundred and fifty big ones a night which worked out pretty great because John had a negative balance of over two hundred and fifty bucks in his bank account. The study was to help people like John with recurring nightmares. It promised to get rid of them once and for all. John would still be miserable, but at least he wouldn't be suicidal. Hooray!

Inside the big grey building there were walls painted grey, grey couches, grey ceiling fans, paintings of grey horses and grey kittens and grey elephants and other grey animals. The staff walking around wore grey clothes. John wondered if they'd give him grey clothes to wear. Grey was his favorite color. He wondered if they knew that about him. He doubted it.

He checked in with the lady at the front desk, gave her his name. She handed him a brick of paperwork with little stickers that pointed to every place he needed to sign or initial. "Make sure you go through this and sign off on everything," she said. "If you have any questions about anything, someone will be here soon to discuss it with you."

But John didn't read any of the paperwork because he didn't really care. He just thought about the idea of never dreaming that dream again. Bye-bye, dumbass dream! Burn in hell!

He signed and initialed. His hand cramped a bit. He fantasized about what his life would be like after the treatment. What dreams would he dream then? He thought about never dreaming again. Maybe that's the real dream.

The lady at the front desk put his paperwork into a tube that got sucked up into the ceiling like, *THWUP!* "You can't bring your phone with you," she said. "There's a telephone in your room that you can use."

He handed it over. "It's dead and I can't find my charger anyway," he said.

Two security guards with flashlights and pepper spray came through the grey metal doors and put John in an elevator with roman numerals for floor numbers, all the way to the top of the building.

"This is exciting," John said to them.

Neither said anything back. The speakers in the elevator played Phil Collins. The song was from the *Face Value* album. John always liked that album. He had forgotten about that album after he started having the dream where he was a skyscraper. After the treatment is over, he thought, I'm gonna listen to a lot more Phil Collins. Yeah.

His room was a little makeshift studio apartment with a kitchen-ette and a desk and a mirror and a toilet and a bed. It was nicer than his actual apartment which wasn't really an apartment and was more or less a 1994 Honda Accord. Life's really all about how you look at it, you know? Luxury is subjective. The rotary phone was on the desk. Guess what color it was.

Once of the guards said, "If you need anything, dial 4," and they left.

John waited for someone to come by and lay down the ground rules of the study. No one did. No worries. All good. John didn't mind, really. He closed his eyes, fell right asleep.

The dream played out as usual. John, a skyscraper. Everyone in the world, happy because of him. Kids laughing. People in love. People living forever, healed and whole. Even God was in a good mood. Halfway through the dream, John did something he'd never done in any previous version of the recurring dream. He got tired. He'd never been tired before but OMG he was so tired this time. No matter how hard he fought it, his enormous skyscraper eyes just couldn't stay open. The yawn he let out caused a tidal wave on the east coast. Comets fell from space, landing in the shape of a perfectly firm mattress. And it was heated. Everyone who lived inside of John kept saying, go on and get some rest, buddy. We'll be here when you wake up. We're fine. Don't worry about us. Etc. Etc. So, he laid down and went to sleep.

When John woke up, he couldn't see anything. He couldn't see anything because there was hair covering his eyes. A shit ton of hair. His hair. It had grown out. It had grown out several feet everywhere on his body: on his head, on his face, on his knuckles and toes. John was a hairy motherfucker. His nails were about two feet long, too. And he was really fucking thirsty. He heard a sound fill the space around him. Something like brrrringgggg-brrrrringgggg-brrrrrrinnggggggggggggggg-ggg. He reached over and answered it.

Dust flew out of his lips when he said, "Hello."

"Welcome back," said the phone.

"What time is it?"

"Time is relative."

"What day is it?"

"Today."

"What year is it?"

"You've been asleep for four hundred and ninety years."

John felt heat run up and down his legs. He was pissing himself. He probably hadn't pissed in over four hundred years. Whatever. Let it go, man. Piss away!

"Someone will be there to help you soon."

Two new guards with new clothes and new flashlights came and helped John take his things downstairs. The guards smiled the whole time. Not in a creepy way or anything. In a way that made John feel like they were happy to see him. They even high fived him. Cool!

At the front desk there was a hologram of the woman who had been there when he first checked in. She wasn't smiling. Some things are meant to stay the same forever. She told John that his bank account had been credited with all of the money he had made while remaining the only subject in this study and that he was now a very, very, very rich man. His 1994 Honda Accord was towed and demolished, though. Sorry about it.

"Thanks," he said.

John walked the streets of the new world he had woken up to. There were no more vehicles. People could fly. John could fly! He just thought about it and it happened. Up, up, and away! He popped into a salon and got cleaned up. When it was time to pay, he handed the hair stylist his debit card. She told him debit cards were vintage and probably worth a lot of money. She kissed him on the cheek and said, "Thank you for letting me cut your hair. Come back any time. I love you."

Everywhere he went, people were smiling and laughing and happy. People said hello and how are you and have a good day and you look amazing and I love you and please and may I and thank you and yes, yes, yes, yes, yes!

John found an apartment in the middle of the city. At sunset, he'd sit on the roof of the building and look out at the city. The building overlooked everyone, everything. Beautiful.

John thought about all the things he could do in this new world. He could date, meet someone, get married, start a family, have a hundred grandkids and great grandkids and great-great grandkids and so on. He could find and work a job he enjoyed. He could travel, see the world, take a vacation in another part of the universe. He sat atop his building, dreaming about the future. He dreamed and dreamed and dreamed. He stood on the ledge, closed his eyes, fell backward, ready to sleep again.

Do It Yourself

Look, I know a lot of people like to fake their own deaths for a shit ton of reasons, like they're in debt or wanted for murder or afraid of being parents or whatever. But I'm not that guy. I'm just bored. To be honest, I would really love to actually, literally die. I'm just too chicken shit to kill myself. Also, blood makes me queasy. I don't do drugs so I don't wanna overdose on anything. It kind of sucks that you can't force yourself to die peacefully in your sleep from natural causes. Can you? Still, it would be way cooler to go out with a bang, you know? Like, die in a way that it turns into something all my friends talk about for years to come. Something they'd make a movie about or write a novel about or whatever. Yeah. Something like that.

Anyway, I'm surfing the world wide web when an ad pops up on my screen for a do-it-yourself fake your own death kit. Rad! Sometimes the stars just align, you know? Maybe it's the universe telling me that it also thinks I should die, but it's not quite ready for me to *die* die just yet, you know? I hear you loud and clear, universe!

So, yeah, I buy it. It says it'll be here in 5-7 business days. Okay. I can manage that.

For 5-7 business days, I sit on my couch and count the dust particles floating around my living room. I get up to one hundred thousand or so. I lose count, start over. Good times. I wait for the mailman, wait to see if today is the day he'll deliver my kit. Each day another disappointment.

One day he knocks on my door. I open the door, snatch everything out of his hands. False alarm. It's only coupons to Costco, Petco, Home

Depot, and credit card offers from J. Crew, Discover, Costco, Petco, and Home Depot. See, this is why.

"Take forever," I say.

He goes, "What are you waiting for?"

"A new beginning," I say.

He squints his eyes all funny-like.

Part of me feels like I shouldn't have said that. Like I just gave away a clue or something for the FBI or CIA or USPS to figure out that I faked my own death and throw me in the slammer. I need to throw him off my trail. No, wait. Shit. I need him to deliver my mail because the kit is coming in the mail. Duh. I'm an amateur lol!

"Just kidding," I say. "I'm not going anywhere. I'm going to live forever!"

The kit arrives. It's bigger than I thought it would be. Like, four by four or something like that. It's wrapped very discretely. The sender's address is marked like this:

None of Your Business

Stay in Your Lane Drive

Your Mom's Butt, CA. 666

I love it. It sends the right message: mind your own bee's wax. No one would suspect a thing. And that's the thing. For no one to suspect that I'm going to fake my own death. No one will ever know. Just me and my secret living forever, getting away from this shitty life of monotony and misery. See ya!

I'm so excited to open the kit that I gag just a little bit. Nothing crazy, just a little. Whatever. It's fine.

I use my bare hands trying to rip off the tape but the tape is too strong or I'm too weak so my house keys will work just fine. The keys cut jaggedly into the tape. As the box opens, I see a light coming from inside. I hear voices, too. Hard to make out what they're saying. After the major flaps are properly eviscerated by my car keys, I open the box and a ladder pops out. At the top of the ladder there's a sticky note stickied that says *Someone will be with you shortly*. Sweet! The ladder starts moving. Someone is climbing up. His red hair pokes through the opening in the box.

"Dave!"

"Carl?" I haven't seen Carl since he got expelled from high school after flushing concrete down the toilets in the guy's restroom.

Carl says, "It's great seeing you, dude. I recognized your name on my list but wasn't sure if it was you or another Dave with your last name. Stoked to see you, bro!"

"I thought you got blown up in a meth lab?"

Carl gives me this smile like, bro, you don't even know. Some of his teeth were missing. Like, a lot of them. The whole bottom left.

"Nah, man! I mean, yeah I was cooking and shit but my mom found out and forced me to go to rehab. After that, I worked some temp jobs doing shit like janitorial services, cleaning the washers and dryers at laundromats. You know, whatever. Then I met my homie Aaron and he hooked me up with a job helping people fake their own deaths. It's, like, real rewarding. Been here ever since"

He looks legitimately happy. He doesn't smell like cigarettes and Hot Pockets like he did in high school. His clothes are still way too big for him. The crack of his flat ass reaching out of his Dickies like the hand on that Evil Dead poster. Everyone's got a thing.

"I'm happy for you, man. I'm glad it's you helping me fake my own death."

Carl walked me through the plan. He and I would sneak out the back and hop in the van that was waiting for us. I was allowed to bring one thing. Only one thing. I thought about either my Knicks hat that I've had since I was a kid or my mom's ashes. Once we were in the van, he'd give me all my new paperwork. If there was something about my backstory or my new location or name or whatever that I didn't like, tough shit. You get what you get.

"You good with that?" Carl asks.

"For sure."

Another guy climbs out of the box. He looks like the goth version of Guy Fieri. Goth Fieri.

Carl says, "This is Albert. He's gonna be your body double."

I ask what that means.

Albert says, "Means when they find 'your' body, it'll actually be my body. Can't fake your own death without a body, dude."

"Don't worry, man," Carl says, "Albert is immortal. After a few days, his ashes will do this thing where they kind of find each other and reconnect. It's rad but also kinda gross."

Albert makes the devil horns with both hands like, fuck yeah.

I do the devil horns back like, sounds good.

Carl is rocking back and forth on his heels, ready to explode, checking his watch every few seconds. It's one of those watches that's really just an obnoxiously large leather band with a clock in the middle. Cool.

Albert walks around the house, studying like he'll need to remember it. Like someone will ask his temporarily dead body for important details to prove that he's not him, that he's really me. Who am I to question his methods?

Carl asks if I'm ready.

"I just need to grab my one thing." I grab my Knicks hat. "Let's go," I say.

The dude driving the van hands me a manila envelope containing my new life. Carl tells him to drive up to the top of the street so we can watch my house, my memories, my old life blow up. The driver is cool, says no problemo.

We sit on top of the van, overlook my street. The moon turns brighter and the sky turns blacker, its outer edges a burnt orange. An ice cream truck coasts through the neighborhood in neutral, music warbling from a megaphone that's older than me. The song is Goo by Sonic Youth. Cool. A few local homeless people ride in their shopping carts down the sidewalk, race one another. Yellowed teeth, all smiles. Good times. They go through the trash set out on the street, share with one another. Children sit in their lawns, make sculptures from old toys while their parents smoke weed and drink wine. You remember things the way you want.

Carl goes, "Helluva view."

"Yeah, it's not bad," I say.

A sound like KA-BOOM goes off from inside my house. The fire reaches toward heaven, sends Albert straight to hell. It's like the creation of the universe. Or the end of it. Whatever works.

I pick up the manila folder with my new life, feel how light it is. That's a good sign. Less baggage, you know? I can start over, rebuild. The future is mine! Maybe this is better than dying. Maybe the universe is right and literally killing myself isn't the answer. Maybe it's better to just sort of kill myself, or an idea of myself. Introducing the new me to the universe. Here I am. The new me. Things will be better this time. I'll be better. Happier. More productive.

I take one last glance back at my old life, breathe in the new possibilities.

A toilet lid flies up from the explosion, goes straight through my face, tears my head in two.

The Same Two Songs

I'm jerking off in the shower the first time I see my dad's ghost. He doesn't see me trip over the tub onto the carpet, cupping my junk. But there he is: heavy black bags under his eyes, a galaxy of freckles stretched out and connected, giving the illusion of a tan, bald head, red and white beard. He stares blankly into the clouded mirror above my sink, turns and walks through the bathroom door. I wait on the front porch for mom to get home before going back inside.

"I saw dad in the bathroom," I say.

"You're grieving," she says.

She used to give him shit over everything. Like buying a riding lawn mower instead of a push kind or grilling her steak rarer than she wanted.

She'd go, "Ah, shit, Jerry, what the hell is wrong with you? You trying to kill me?"

He'd laugh, "Everyone knows you're gonna kill me first, Debra."

Now when someone asks how she's doing she just says, "He was a great man, and he was my husband."

I'm taking a leak in the middle of the night the next time I see him. I pass out, wake up soaked in piss. He's still there, silently staring at himself in the mirror. I try to get his attention, throw my arms around and shit. Just like last time, he turns and walks through the closed door. I wait for him to come back for a while, wondering how to get him to see me. If I stand where he stood, what would happen? But the idea of accidentally being possessed by the spirit of my dad scares the shit out

of me and makes me nauseous. I try taking the mirror off the wall. It
doesn't budge. I give up, go back to bed.

I wonder where he goes when he isn't haunting me. Like, is there
a ghost dad rock band where they only play covers of Live and Super-
tramp. I feel like that'd be something he'd be into. When I was a kid, he
used to pull out this old guitar his dad gave him, tune it up, and strum.
Always the same two songs. His calloused thumb scratched against
the worn dull steel strings while his other hand fumbled to form the
only three chords he knew. I'd stand in the doorway and listen. After
finishing the songs, he tucked the guitar in the closet behind his coats,
found me standing there. He said when I got older and could hold the
guitar, he'd teach me what he knew.

If mom is having any similar paranormal experiences, she doesn't
mention them. I also haven't asked. She spends most of her time now
decorating the living room with houseplants. They hang from the
ceilings and stand in every corner.

I'm helping her hang shelves for the succulents when I slip. A few
plants crash and spill onto the floor. She goes, "Ah, shit, Jerry!" I wait
for her to acknowledge that she called me by his name. She doesn't.
It's like she doesn't care. I lose it. I pick up one of the small pots and
chuck it across the room, covering the walls in black dirt and cacti. She
freezes. My voice booms throughout the house. A parade of insults and
obscenities cascade out of my mouth. Halfway through my rant, she
slaps me across my face.

"Your father never would have let you talk to me like that," she says.
It takes a second, but it comes hard and fast.

I'm blubbering.

She grabs me by the back of my neck, puts my head on her shoulders. I wail until my throat goes raw. She holds me for a long time,
runs her fingers through my hair, lets me go on. "You're just like him,"
she whispers.

We sob as we clean, our faces wet and stinging, hands caked in dirt. I vacuum the last bit of soil off the carpet, go into my bathroom and start a shower. Steam rises and drifts across the ceiling, fogging the edges of the mirror. I study my reflection, see my father looking back at me.

Tacos

I get my ass kicked one night while I'm delivering some tacos to this dude in Pomona. The restaurant I work for doesn't even do anything about it. They say because no one was caught on camera or captured by the cops or put on social media or whatever, their hands are tied. What they meant to say is, "We think you're a fucking liar and you're just trying to get free money from us." On top of that, I never finish delivering the tacos. I'm too busy bleeding from my nose and mouth and asshole. My bad. The really shitty thing is that the people who kick my ass don't even take my money or the tacos. They crack my skull because it's fun. For them. Not for me. It isn't fun at all for me.

The first few days after it happens, I live in my bathtub. I eat, sleep, get drunk, piss and shit in my bathtub. It's hard to feel safe anywhere in this world anymore. At least in my bathtub I feel protected. No one can get me in my porcelain fortress. The world is a world away. My new home holds me like a little baby. It keeps me safe, keeps my alive. I don't mind sleeping in the fetal position. I don't mind waffle stomping my turds. All of it totally fine by me. No complaints whatsoever. This is my new normal.

My friend, Eve, shows up after a few weeks of that, though, and says, "Get up, Glen. You're being a pussy."

"I am a pussy," I say.

She opens her bag, pulls out everything inside. Candles. Salt. Lace. Book of spells. Mason jar filled with blood. Knives.

"What's this for?"

"I'm helping," she says. "Now get the fuck out of the tub."

We push everything in my living room against the walls, make a circle with the salt. Eve draws symbols inside and outside of the circle using the jar of blood. I don't know what they mean. We stand in the middle of the circle, hold hands.

She closes her eyes and goes, "We call upon you, Dark Lord Keven. My friend needs you. Rise up from your throne of skulls and give him the strength to go out into the world again and fuck up the assholes who turned him into the piece of shit he is now."

"Dude, that's harsh."

She takes the knife and makes a huge gash across the innermost part of her palm. "Open your mouth," she says.

"Serious?"

"Goddammit, Glen!"

I open my mouth. She squeezes her hand, blood drips down the back of my throat, tastes like maple syrup. Okay. Better than I expected.

Eve keeps going, "Lord Keven, make your presence known."

We wait. Nothing happens. The neighbors are listening to some emo music. Blech. Gross.

I go "Did you do it right?"

"Yeah, dumbass." She reaches for the spell book and BLAM! The book goes up in flames six feet high. An electric guitar wails around us. All the light from the room disappears. The circle of salt rises high in the air, comes together to form the most frighteningly badass creature I've ever seen. It's like a buffalo fucked an anaconda and a dragon.

"'Sup, fuckers," Keven says, his voice like what I imagine hell to sound like. Rad.

Eve falls on her face, fangirls hard. "It's really you," she says.

Keven grabs me by my throat, pulls me in so we're face to face. Blood drips from his mouth. Bits of raw human flesh stuck between black teeth. I bet no one would steal tacos from Keven. He sticks out his tongue—it's forked, obviously—wipes my face with it.

He asks, "What do you want?"

"I don't know," I say.

"Then why the fuck am I here?"

Eve stands up. "Lord Keven? Glen got his ass kicked a couple of weeks ago and is too afraid to leave the bathtub. He just needs some confidence, to know how to handle himself if he runs into trouble again."

Keven drops me. I fall to the floor, crumble like a paper man. He takes his tail, thrusts it into my skull. My entire existence replays in his demon brain. He learns everything about me. It gives me a gooey feeling throughout my body. Like, it's not uncomfortable or anything, but it's definitely super evil. I'm for sure going to hell now.

Eve says, "I'll give you anything you want."

I sign the contract containing the terms of our agreement with a pen made from a human femur, which is way more difficult than it sounds. I have to hold it up with both hands because you can't exactly place it comfortably between two fingers. The ink is my blood, duh.

Once the agreement is signed and everything, Keven says we should celebrate. Head out for a night on the town. Fuck some shit up. Paint the city red or however that saying goes.

"I'd love to," Eve says.

"Sounds fun," I say.

"Dope," Keven says.

We steal our shitty emo neighbors' Toyota Corolla and head to the city. Keven takes out a Ziploc bag of coke. We take turns sticking our whole heads inside, breathing deeply. I can't feel my anything LOL!

Eve and Keven are making out in the backseat when the red and blue lights start flashing behind us. Keven tells me to pull over. Okay.

Two cops approach the Corolla with their guns drawn. One of them goes, "What in the flying fuck is wrong with you? You almost ran us over half a mile back. Are you fucking high?"

Keven bursts through the Corolla's roof. The cops piss themselves, start shooting. Eve is cackling like a maniac. I'm trying to remember my name.

I don't see it exactly, but there's some screaming and some oh my god oh my god, please no please no, and a loud squelch, then the cops go quiet.

We're in the cop car, Keven is driving. I'm making the wee-ooo wee-ooo sound with my mouth. Or maybe it's the actual sirens? I don't know. Eve's face is made of diamonds now. She says she's never felt so pretty.

Keven says, "Yeah, baby, you're so fucking hot. Come here."

We're at Red Robin. I order every hamburger on the menu. Keven is eating the waiter's face. Eve is throwing up on her fries.

"Best night ever," she says.

There's a cover band at the bar. They're playing 90s music. Keven asks the lead singer if the band knows any Cake.

Before Keven starts singing the third track from Prolonging the Magic, he spits in my and Eve's mouths. Everything turns into a cartoon. I'm a bear and Eve is an ostrich. Keven is still a lord of hell, just a cartoon version. The band are Muppets. The bartenders are spiders, serving venom. The whole bar is in the midst of a giant orgy as Keven sings his demon heart out.

Eve and I wake up in my bathtub. We're the kind of hungover where nothing hurts but nothing feels right either. The mason jar of blood is empty. A line of salt formed around the tub. The knife broken.

Eve grabs her things, puts them in her bag.

"Later," she says.

"Ok."

I leave the bathtub, go back out into the world. I feel good. I get back to work, find a job as a chef for a little Mexican restaurant. Over the years, I work my way up. The owners die, leave the restaurant to me. Their kids are pissed. LMAO! I'm CEO, motherfucker. The restaurant expands, spreads out across California, the United States, the whole world. We're Fortune 500, baby. Presidents and oligarchs and dictators and movie stars and celebrities and mobsters and Guy Fieri all want to eat at my restaurant. A few of them owe me favors. They find the guys who kicked my ass. I handle it.

Business is good. Everyone loves my tacos. No matter how much time passes or how differently the meat is prepared, it always looks exactly like it did between Keven's teeth.

Remember To Breathe

Before he leaves his therapist's office, his therapist tells him to remember to breathe. To close his eyes, breathe in through his nose, out through his mouth. To focus on his breath. The way the air feels going in. The way it feels leaving. This is supposed to help him stay in the moment. It's supposed to help him realize that, in the moment, there is no present danger. That he's okay. That everything is going to be okay. Even if it may not seem that way. It's like he's breathing in all the positive, breathing out the negative.

He shoots his therapist a thumbs up like, you got it, dude.

He pops in the liquor store by his house, decides to get a tall can. Doesn't matter which. Any will do. He probably won't even drink it. He just wants to hold it. It makes him feel good. Makes him feel tougher than he really is.

The cashier starts screaming. Someone else is screaming, too. Some other people are also screaming. Everyone is screaming. AAGGGH-HHH!!! Or something. He peaks his head out from behind the rack with the donuts and the protein bars—which are essentially the same thing—sees someone pointing a sawed-off shotgun at the cashier.

The gunman goes, "Gimme all your fucking money or I'll fucking blow your fucking brains out all over this fucking piece of shit store!"

The cashier goes, "AAAGGGHHH!!!"

He drops the tallboy of Keystone Light. It goes kssshhhhhh all over the dirty laminate floor.

A second gunman comes from around the corner, pulls out another sawed-off shotgun and points it at him. The second gunman says, "Don't move."

He doesn't move. Can't move. Even if he wanted to. His body is frozen. Turned solid. Except the little bit of piss dribbling down his leg. Whoops. How embarrassing.

His whole life flashes before his eyes. He thinks about the time he went headfirst into a mailbox when he was learning to ride a bike and how that lead him to never learn how to ride a bike. He thinks about that time he got a boner in eighth grade, and everyone saw it and got grossed out and pointed and laughed, and the teacher saw it and couldn't help but laugh herself. He thought about his wedding day. How he never had one because he's still a virgin and no one has ever loved him. He thought about how after his head is blown off by the second gunman, his cats back in his apartment would probably starve to death because no one would think to check on them because he had no friends and no family.

Between the cashier crying and the gunman screaming and the second gunman pointing a gun in his face, it surprises him that he remembers what his therapist told him about remembering to breathe. The fact that he even remembers what his therapist had told him about breathing causes him to feel a little proud of himself which never happens. He never feels proud of himself. Now he's proud for feeling a sense of pride. Shit. Now he feels a little guilty because who is he kidding? He's about to die and no one will care. Boo hoo.

He thinks about breathing. Takes a deep breath in. Real deep. Like, filling his lungs to the brim with whatever oxygen and dead skin is floating around him. He exhales, blows every last bit of air out. He takes another breath, lets it out. And another, and out again. The more he breathes, the better he feels. As his head expands and the world outside feels a million miles away, he hears the second gunman shouting what the fuck! what the fuck! what the fuck! As the screaming continues, the cold steel of the sawed-off shotgun massages his nasal passages, settling in his lungs like a baby finally going to sleep after hours of hard crying. He opens his eyes. The whole store is watching him, eyes wide, jaws dropped.

Keep breathing.

In and out.

Just like that.

With every breath, he takes something in the liquor store with him. The second gunman's shotgun is gone. The first gunman's shotgun comes next. The first gunman holds on to the register for dear life as the atoms or molecules or whatever in his body stretch out across the store and go swirly whirly into our hero's nostrils and goodbye, gone, see ya never! The second gunman tries to run for it. No luck. Later, gator!

The cashier starts cheering. Everyone outside watching through the windows starts cheering. The police show up, start cheering. The neighborhood children start cheering. He's hoisted on the shoulders of complete strangers. They parade him around the city. Roses and twenty-dollar bills and women's underwear and men's underwear are thrown to him. Someone brings him his cats. The cats tell him how proud they are of him. How they've always been proud of him. How lucky they are to belong to him and no one else. A memorial is made in his honor. The city is renamed after him.

He breathes and breathes and breathes deep and heavy, removing all the evil in the world, bottling it all inside himself, sheltering the world from everything that could hurt it. He takes it.

Heroes

Angel shouts from the front lawn fifteen feet below, "Prove it!"

I go, "I'm gonna!" I look out at the other houses on my street. The roof is quiet. The neighbor's brown and black labs sit behind the fence in a calm anticipation for whatever comes next. Good dogs. A woodpecker barrels away in a tree somewhere nearby. The oil stain Dad's Corolla left in the driveway looks like an outline of one of the characters on Sesame Street, I don't remember which one. It's ninety degrees with no breeze, but still much cooler than any other day that summer. Summer's almost over. In a few weeks I start seventh grade and Angel will be in high school, leaving me for a different school. Other kids' older brothers might treat them like shit, but Angel isn't one of those older brothers. He's chill. Better than chill. The best.

One day after lunch, this kid, Roger Roberts, cornered me in the bathroom and started calling me "Horse Boy" because, when I smile, my upper lip goes up higher than normal and shows the gums above my teeth. Roger neighed and laughed neighed and laughed neighed and laughed until the other boys joined in. Angel walked in, saw me crying, shoved Roger against the wall. "I'll rip your nuts out through your fucking mouth and feed them to your cunt mother if you ever talk to my brother again." Roger and the other boys don't bother me anymore.

"You can't fly, Danny," Angel says, his hand cupped over his eyes to block the sun.

"Yes I can!"

"No you can't. And if you fall and break your arm, don't you dare blame me when Mom and Dad get home."

"I'm not gonna fall and I'm not gonna break my arm. I'm going to fly! You'll see." Anxiety builds in my chest. My windpipe thins and no matter how much air I suck back, my lungs feel empty.

"Then do it already or I'm going back inside."

I open my mouth to scream at him and almost lose my balance. I shuffle back across the brown shingles and wipe the sweat from my palms on the back of my shorts.

Angel laughs. "Don't kill yourself, Danny."

"What am I going to do if Roger Roberts tries to mess with me this year and you're not there? He'll kick my ass."

Angel drops his head and stares at our overgrown grass, then looks up at me without shielding his eyes. "If Roger Roberts tries anything at all, I'll go straight to his house and beat the shit out of him and his dad. And you can tell him I said that."

"You promise?"

"I swear."

I believe him.

A red minivan creeps up in front of our house. Mrs. Daschbach, one of the blue-haired ladies that lives down the street, yells from the window, "What are you doing up there, boy?"

"I accidentally threw a Frisbee on the roof. Danny's just getting it for me," Angel lies.

"Well, get down before you fall and break something."

"Yes, ma'am. He's coming down now." Angel lies better than me, but no one else knew that. People accuse me of lying all the time: teachers, parents, neighbors, the kids in class, the therapist Mom and Dad sent me to.

I wave at Mrs. Daschbach as she drives away. She gives me a you're-up-to-something kinda look.

Angel turns back to me, "I'm going inside."

"No! Wait. I'm ready."

"Danny, just get down. It's not funny anymore. You're going to get hurt."

"No, I'm not!" I take three giant steps backward, take off running across the roof of our house, crouch down and spring into the airspace over our front lawn. My body is weightless as I float above Angel who's screaming holy shit holy shit holy fucking shit and turning circles like a dog chasing its tail. I arch by back and position myself like Superman watching over Earth from space. The dogs next door bark frantically. The gums above my teeth are on full display.

I look up and see my mom's car turn down the street. My body weighs over a thousand pounds. I crash hard face-first into the ground below me, black out.

The sun falls just behind the skyline when I wake up in the hospital room. I try to move my arms but the casts around them won't budge. My left eye is swollen shut and I taste blood in my mouth. Angel shoots up from the chair in the corner, rushes to my side.

"Hey, you okay?"

"Yeah, I'm okay. Where's Mom and Dad?"

"Dad went to get us food and Mom is outside on the phone." Angel closes the door, pulls his chair next to me. "Danny, you can fly," he says, keeping his voice real low.

"I told you I could." My gums are showing again. It hurts to smile but I don't care.

"Fuck yeah, you did. I'm sorry I didn't believe you."

"It's okay. Did you tell Mom and Dad what happened?"

"I told them what I told Mrs. Dashbach—you went up for a Frisbee, slipped, and fell."

I stare at my brother's face, seeing how proud he (anyone) is of me, like I'm his hero. He's mine.

"Don't worry. I won't tell anyone. I swear."

I go, "No."

"No what?"

"Tell everyone."

Whoosh

I wanted my funeral to be like one of those drive-thru car washes where they set my casket on some rollers or whatever and wheel me through a long glass tunnel. So, when I died, they modeled my funeral after one of those drive-thru car washes. Pretty killer, man. Now I'm propped up on a bunch of pillows in my casket, drinking a cold beer, and waving to everyone who's either crying or laughing or I can't tell which because their faces kinda look the same either way.

Goodbye, friends!

Goodbye, family!

Goodbye, property taxes and freeway traffic and electricity bills and blah blah blah!

It's onward for me.

At the end of the tunnel there's this big hole where I'll fall down, down, down until I reach the afterlife or wind up in the future where everyone is made of sunshine or metal or something. I take one last look at the world and *whoosh*! The wind blows through my dead hair and I'm off to eternity.

The casket almost topples over as it lands back on the rollers. Everyone except my family is gone.

My wife goes, "What the fuck are you doing?"

I shrug.

I try to get out of the casket. My legs don't work anymore. Bummer. But there's a fresh beer in my hand and Stone Temple Pilots are playing and my wife is still here so it ain't all bad. I reach the end of the tracks, tell my wife I love her (again), go down the hole.

Songs: Ohia is playing in the tunnel this time. My wife is there, but she's older. Like, ten or fifteen years older. She's got grey in her brown hair, wrinkles brushed around her eyes. She's wearing my Wrangler shirt and drinking a PBR. I love her even more now that I'm dead.

"They cured cancer," she says.

"I didn't have cancer," I say.

"No, but it's still pretty cool."

"You're right. I love you!"

"See you soon!"

My wife flashes me her tits. They're old, like her. She's still got it, though.

Whoosh.

The trees outside the tunnel have grown over a thousand feet tall. They're filled with bluebirds and jaybirds and parakeets and basically all kinds of birds. My wife is asleep in her wheelchair. I try not to wake her as I crack open my beer.

Whoosh.

Snow is falling in soft white blankets like dreams coming to children for the first time. My wife isn't here. Damien Jurado is singing "The Last Great Washington State". It's a song about leaving. My favorite song, actually. I wonder why I ever left. I miss my wife, my kids.

Whoosh.

The lights are off in the car wash funeral. No music. The wheels barely spin anymore. They creek. The beer is stale.

Whoosh.

The car wash funeral is free-floating in space. Everything that's ever existed is gone.

"You're back," she says.

She's behind me, in her own casket with her own wheels, and two fresh beers.

"You're back," I say.

We drift out into nothingness, together, getting drunk and making out and listening to whatever music is left in the void.

Whoosh.

D.T. Robbins works and lives in Southern California with his wife and kids. He is founding editor of Rejection Letters. Hello!

Printed in the USA
CPSIA information can be obtained
at www.ICGtesting.com
LVHW101037281223
767436LV00066B/2031